Amos Tutuola

The Wild Hunter

in the Bush of the Ghosts

Edited by Bernth Lindfors

Three Continents Press

3CP

Washington, D.C.

©Amos Tutuola 1989

First Standard Version

Three Continents Press
1636 Connecticut Avenue, N.W.
Washington, D.C. 20009

Facsimile Edition ©Three Continents Press, 1982

Library of Congress Cataloging-in-Publication Data:

Tutuola, Amos.
   The wild hunter in the Bush of the Ghosts / Amos Tutuola;
edited by Bernth Lindfors.—1st standard version.
    p.   cm.
ISBN 0-89410-452-7 — ISBN 0-89410-453-5 (pbk.)
1. Yoruba (African people)—Folklore—Fiction. I. Lindfors,
Bernth. II. Title.
[PR9387.9.T8W45 1989]
823—dc20   84-51444
                                   CIP

All rights reserved. No part of this book
may be used or reproduced in any manner
whatsoever without written permission of the
publisher except for brief quotations in
reviews or articles.

Cover art and illustrations by Max K. Winkler
©Three Continents Press, 1989

Foreword

Amos Tutuola wrote this story in 1948. It was his first attempt at writing a long narrative for publication, and after submitting it to a publisher in London, he went on to write *The Palm-Wine Drinkard and His Dead Palm-Wine Tapster in the Deads' Town* (1952), the book that made him famous throughout the world. The curious history of *The Wild Hunter*'s circuitous journey into print has been told at some length in a facsimile edition of the original manuscript published by Three Continents Press in 1982, so it is unnecessary to repeat it here. but the reader should be aware that this tale is a young raconteur's initial venture into a written mode of storytelling.

When Amos Tutuola came to the United States in the fall of 1983 to participate in the International Writers' Workshop at the University of Iowa, he was invited by Three Continents Press to prepare a new edition of *The Wild Hunter* for wider circulation. He went through the typescript of the original version carefully, correcting obvious errors and restructuring several episodes. I was asked to lend a hand in the revision and to supervise computerized typesetting of the final text. So what is being presented here is basically the same old *Wild Hunter* in more modern dress. This tranformation, achieved by means of the latest technological miracles, is very much in keeping with the spirit of the story. We hope you enjoy this retold tale.

Bernth Lindfors

The Wild Hunter in the Bush of Ghosts is the first long prose fiction written for publication in English by a Nigerian author, a fitting harbinger of the rich and varied literary efflorescence to follow. Amos Tutuola must be recognized as a founding father of one of the most remarkable national literatures to emerge in an international language in the 20th century. His first work deserves a place of ancestral honor in the pantheon not only of Nigerian letters but of African writing.

The work, although written in 1948, was published for the first time in 1982 by Three Continents Press in a limited edition that reproduced the manuscript opposite a typescript version. A long chain of events is reponsible for this 34-year time lag: once down on school-pad paper, the manuscript was sent off to Mr. A. Kraszna-Krausz, Director of Focal Press in London, who, intrigued by Tutuola's offer of photographs of ghosts which were to accompany the work, had asked to see it.

Though disappointed to discover the photographs were only of drawings of ghosts, Kraszna-Krausz believed the 77-page manuscript deserved some compensation and purchased rights. But the work languished unpublished for long years and only Tutuola's occasional vague references to his "first" novel kept the matter at all public. Only in the last few years did a newly opened trail through the files of Faber and Faber in search of the equally long-lost manuscript of *The Palm-Wine Drinkard* (Tutuola's first published work [1952]) lead to the elusive manuscript of *The Wild Hunter in the Bush of Ghosts*.

When Amos Tutuola came to the United States in the fall of 1983, he was invited by Three Continents Press to prepare a new edition of *The Wild Hunter* for wider circulation. He went through the typescript of the original version carefully, correcting obvious errors and restructuring several episodes. Bernth Lindfors, professor of African and English literature at the University of Texas at Austin, assisted in the revision. This edition presents the same old *Wild Hunter* in more modern dress, a transformation that has remained very much in keeping with the spirit of the story.

First Standard Edition
Three Continents Press
1636 Connecticut Avenue NW
Washington, D.C. 20009

ISBN: 0-89410-452-7 (cloth);
453-5 (paper)
LC No.: 84-51445

Other Three Continents Books of Related Interest

Amadou Hampâté Bâ *Kaidara* (translated by Daniel Whitman)
Nafissatou Diallo *Fary, Princess of Tiali* (translated by Ann Woollcombe)
Emil Magel *Folktales from the Gambia*
Jean Price-Mars *So Spoke the Uncle* (translated by Magdalene Shannon)
Norman Simms *Oral and Traditional Literatures*
Ellis Singano *Tales of Old Malawi*
Marie Tollerson *Mythology and Cosmology in the Narratives of Bernard Dadié and Birago Diop*
Keith Q. Warner *Kaiso! The Trinidad Calypso*
Richard Winstedt *Malay Proverbs*
René Philombe *Tales from Cameroon*

Table of Contents

Foreword by Bernth Lindfors/iii

Biographical and Bibliographical Information on
Three Continents' Limited Edition of Holograph Version/iv

The Story of the Wild Hunter's Father/1
The First Town of the Ghosts/14
The Second Town of the Ghosts/33
The Third Town of the Ghosts/44
The Fourth Town of the Ghosts/62
The Fifth Town of the Ghosts/91
    Our First Day in the Fifth Town/92
    Our Second Day in the Fifth Town/93
    Our Third Day in the Fifth Town/94
    Our Fourth Day in the Fifth Town/95
    Our Fifth Day in the Fifth Town/97
    Our Sixth Day in the Fifth Town/99

Our Way to Heaven/108
    Our First Day in Heaven/119
    Our Second Day in Heaven/120
    Our Third Day in Heaven/120
    Our Fourth Day in Heaven/121
    Our Fifth Day in Heaven/121
    Our Sixth Day in Heaven/122
    We Leave Heaven on the Sixth Day/124

Drawings by Max Winkler

The Story of the Wild Hunter's Father

One midnight my father, who was a hunter by profession, woke me and asked me to sit down in front of him. He said, "My son, I want you to listen attentively to what I am going to tell you, because I am now old and I feel that I will soon respond to the call of God to rest." Then, with a very weary voice, he began his story thus:

"I started hunting when I was fifteen years old. Within two years, I had killed several big animals, including elephants, tigers, lions and so many others that I cannot remember all their names now.

"One day, at about two o'clock in the afternoon, I left home for a certain bush which was near our town. After I had journeyed for four hours, I reached this bush just as it was getting a little dark, and I stopped near the bank of a flowing river. I made a fire there, and cut some plantains from plantain trees that were planted along both banks of the river, this being a place that favored the growth of plantains. I roasted four of the plantains in the fire, finishing my dinner at about eight o'clock. Then I went to the river and drank water to my satisfaction.

"When I returned, I sat near the fire and began to plan how I could go deep into the bush and find some animals to kill. But just then, there appeared a ghost with one leg, who was very fat and black like coal-tar. He seemed not to have taken a bath for the past forty years, for his body was smelling badly. He could not walk but was jumping because he had only one leg which was as big as a log of wood. When I saw him leaping toward me, I was frightened and got ready to run away for my life. I knew that even though I had plenty of juju, I could not fight this fearful one-legged ghost.

"As he came near me, he shouted at me horribly, 'What are you doing on my land? Or don't you know that I am the owner of this land? I am the one-legged ghost whom God drove away from heaven because I was worrying his angels. I am the very one God is punishing every day, yet I never abide by His laws and orders. It is over two hundred years now that God has been warring against me. But I am still looking for ways to become even worse than ever.' After shouting like this for a few minutes, the one-legged ghost told me to stand up and follow him to his house.

"All the while, I was considering using one of my spells to turn myself into a big tree so that he might not be able to catch me. But then I saw some other bad spirits who surrounded me suddenly, and I was sure that if I dared to fight with them, they would kill me immediately. In great confusion and fear I used one of my spells to turn myself, my gun and my hunting bag into a big tree, but a few minutes later I saw to my horror that these spirits were preparing a big fire round the foot of that tree (me). When I felt the heat of the fire, I turned from a tree into a sea-worm and flew into the water that was nearby. To my surprise, these spirits followed me into the river, and as I was moving with the current, one of them stretched out his hand, gripped me and then threw me into his mouth. But he did not swallow me. Though my gun was in my hand and my hunting bag and matchet were on my shoulder, I could use neither weapon. His mouth was so hot that I felt that I was in a fire. As I was wondering how to escape from the prison of his mouth, suddenly I found myself in a strange house.

"Later it was clear to me that this house belonged to the one-legged ghost. But now I no longer saw the spirit who had put me into his mouth nor any of his colleagues. All of them had disappeared. All I saw was the one-legged ghost a few feet in front of me, sitting on a big snake which was about two feet long and eight feet in diameter. It was just like a big tree stump, and it had a short head of many different colors. To my horror, I found myself sitting on the skeleton head of a man with many small snakes surrounding me. All were hissing horribly in unison with that big one on which the ghost sat. All these small snakes were serving the one-legged ghost, following him wherever he went and adoring him as though he were their lord.

"But what surprised me most there, my son," my father continued, "was that I discovered a snake tied round my neck so tightly that I could not move even a little from the skeleton head on which I sat. After some hours I was hungry for food and wondering how I could get something to eat. Then a snake pushed in front of me a man's skull containing dead toads and different kinds of worms. This snake was expecting me to eat all this dead rubbish, and the other snakes around me were looking at me anxiously. I had never even tasted toads or worms in my life and thought perhaps they were meant as food for these spirits, but then one of them took the toads and worms, and while another one forced open my mouth, put all this rubbish deeply into my mouth. You see, my son," my father said bitterly, "I ate the toads and worms by force!"

"But then," my father continued, "after a while, the one-legged ghost disappeared together with those snakes whose duty was to follow him wherever he went. They were his guards and messengers. Although all of them left, the one tied to my neck was still there, hissing terribly, and the mighty one on which the ghost had been seated was also at the same spot, scowling at me terribly. Feeling my life was really in danger, I tried to think of one way or another to escape from this strange house. But suddenly I heard the great horrible shout of the snake tied to my neck, a shout so loud that the whole house shook. Soon those snake guards and snake messengers together with their lord, the one-legged ghost, rushed in, all of them looking at me with half an eye. The one-legged ghost asked the snake tied round my neck, 'Did he want to run away?' 'Yes!' the snake replied in their language. Then, feeling sulky, the one-legged ghost ordered his snake guards to bring me before him. I was terrified when they pushed me near him. The snake guards told me to lie down flatly in front of their lord, but I had hardly laid down when the mighty snake on which he sat began to hum fearfully at me as if it wanted to eat or swallow me.

"Then with fearful voice the one-legged ghost asked me whether I wanted to run away from his house. I replied, 'NO! I only have a fever!' He and his guards said that they did not know what fever was, so I asked if he would allow me to explain. He said, 'Yes' and ordered his guards to untie the snake which was on my neck. Then I explained to him that the cause of my fever was his house which was located in a swamp. I went on to say that the houses of earthly people were built on dry land and not under wet rock like his own. And I told him that if our houses were cold and wet like his was, we had something to make them dry. The one-legged ghost asked me what we used for this purpose. I replied that we always made fire in our houses. Then, with great surprise, he asked me what fire was. I suggested that he give me a chance to illustrate what I meant by the fire. I gathered together in one spot all the large and small dried sticks that were in his house. Then I opened my hunting bag, took out two flinty stones, and as he and his snake guards watched in amazement, I lit up the dried sticks in front of them. I told them all to sit nearby, and they were astonished when they felt the heat of the fire.

"Seeing that they were enjoying themselves, I took a yam from my hunting bag and roasted it in the fire. Cutting it into slices, I distributed the roasted yam among the snake guards and their lord. As they ate it with enthusiasm, I explained that everything that earthly people ate was prepared with fire. They were glad when they heard this, because they had never tried to cook their food before they ate it. And they all became lively when the heat of the fire warmed their bodies up.

"Again, with surprise, they asked me where I got the yam I distributed to them. I told them that I got it from the bush and that if they went into the bush, they too would get a lot of yams there. Without hesitation all of them, including their lord, ran to the nearby bush and started to look for yams. When I saw that they were gone and that there was no snake tied on my neck, I took my gun and hunting bag and walked toward the bush, but I could not find a way to get out of the house and escape. Having pondered the matter for a while, I remembered that one of my spells (juju) would turn me into thick smoke. I used this juju and it turned me into thick smoke which the breeze blew away from this strange house.

"However, those snakes which were the guards and messengers for the one-legged ghost were not snakes at all but simply existed in the form of snakes; they were really ghosts. Instead of finding myself back on the same riverbank from which I had been taken, I found myself among thousands of these ghosts at about one o'clock a.m. All were in their marketplace selling and buying, for it was their market day. When I saw them marketing and saw the whole place full of light, I thought I had been taken to my town by the smoke, and I was very glad. Seeing a woman in front of me, I ran to her happily, embraced her, and greeted her, thinking she was an old woman whom I knew. But instead of accepting my greetings, she shouted horribly, and the other ghosts in the market hastily left their goods and rushed up to me, surrounding me quickly. Earthly people's smell, I learned, was different from that of the ghosts. As they were waving their hands across their faces and trying to avoid breathing in my smell, they were shouting earnestly, 'Thief! Thief!' They called me a thief because all earthly people all over the world were taken to be thieves by the ghosts. After a while they pushed me in front of them, continuing to call me a thief, for they really hated the earthly people.

"After they had arrested me as a thief and led me in shame away from the marketplace, we met an elder ghost who covered his nose and face with his long hair. He stopped us and asked the woman ghostess who held me what was the matter. 'This smelling earthly person came and beat me while I was selling my goods in the market!' the woman shouted. The elder ghost then turned his eyes to me and asked, 'Why did you beat her?' I explained to him that I did not beat her but only greeted and embraced her. 'You greeted her and then you embraced her? But what for?' the elder ghost shouted. In fear and confusion I explained to him that I thought she was the woman of my town! 'Is that so?' he said. 'All right, take him to the den of my lions so they can eat him up!' Then he went away. Without mercy I was taken to the den and pushed inside.

"Fortunately, the lions simply surrounded me and played with me as dogs play with their owners. Since ghosts and ghostesses are able to speak all languages spoken by animals, these ghosts asked the lions why they did not eat me. The lions replied, 'We must not kill or eat him, because whenever we went to his town for animals and did not find any, we used to turn ourselves into men and go to this hunter's house. He always treated us well. When it was dark, he allowed us to sleep in his house till the following day. He is a hunter, and we ourselves are hunters. Hunters must never kill other hunters!'

"After the lions had offered this explanation, the merciless ghosts and ghostesses were so annoyed that they pushed me roughly out of the den and started to beat me. Having done this for a while, they led me to a strange hawk which could not be seen or found in any of the earthly people's towns. In their own language they told the hawk of the offense I had committed. Afterwards they told the hawk to carry me to a certain town and put me into a certain fire there. This fire never quenched in the rainy seasons or the dry season. All these ghosts and ghostesses believed this to be the place from which the sun shone out to the world. I was sure that if this strange hawk did as the ghosts and ghostesses told him, I would not be carried far before I would die. The fire was so great that even if a large stone or piece of iron was thrown in it, that substance would burn into ashes immediately like a dry leaf. Fortunately, this strange hawk replied, 'No! I cannot do any harm to this hunter because I always send my son to his town to catch fowls for me, and this man has never at any time killed him. So for his kindness, I pray, let him go without any punishment!'

"The ghosts and ghostesses were not pleased when the strange hawk declined to carry me to the great fire. They snatched me back with anger and pushed me roughly to the bank of a big river. Having complained to the river as they had to the hawk, they threw me into it with force so that the strong current of the water might carry me away. But to their surprise, this river turned into a big stone suddenly and I stood on it. When I began to wave my hands with a smile, they turned back in order to take me from the stone so they could kill me with their own hands. But the stone hastily turned into a small canoe and carried me away as they watched me sulkily. I fell fast asleep as the canoe carried me along on the surface of the water, for I had not been able to sleep since the day that the one-legged ghost had taken me to his house. From then on, I had fallen into the hands of one ghost or another who troubled me and did not give me time to sleep.

"But what surprised me most was that when I woke, I simply found myself inside my house eating. As I thought over everything that had happened to me in the forests and jungles, I feared greatly. However, I thanked God for saving me from those merciless ghosts and ghostesses who sometimes changed themselves into snakes. Now, my Son, I beg you in the name of God that if you want to be a hunter, be well prepared and carry sufficient juju with you to save yourself from the punishments of ghosts and ghostesses. Ah, don't you see that these ghosts and ghostesses are very bad? For instance, I lived in the bush for six months but I was not allowed to kill even a single animal which I could bring home. Though I had killed uncountable wild animals in several jungles and forests, it was not easy to kill any animal in the bush of ghosts. Take all my juju and carry them with you whenever you go into the bush. Goodbye!"

The First Town of the Ghosts

After my father had related to me his bitter experience of hunting, I was greatly shocked and totally depressed. However, he gave me all his spells, charms, gun and hunting bag, and warned me to take care of them. I prepared his bed for him, for he felt ready to sleep as soon as he had finished telling of his experience with the ghosts. But two hours later, when I went to his room in order to wake him, I found him already dead. Then I and the other family members buried him according to our native form of burial. His funeral ceremony was well attended by the other hunters of the town. That was how my father's story went. Now I have finished the story of my father.

But my own story went as follows. Having thought over the sad experience of my late father as a hunter, I greatly feared becoming a hunter. And when I considered the future life of those new hunters who were yet to come, I was very sorry for them. It was when I was twenty years of age that my father died.

Three months after his death, I started to hunt with the gun, hunting bag, spells and charms which I inherited from him.

One day, at about four o'clock in the evening, I took my father's gun and hunting bag, which I filled with some coco-yams and all the spells and charms he left for me. Then I went to a certain bush which was twelve miles away from the town, arriving there at nine o'clock in the night. But since I was tired, I stopped under a small tree before going further. I leaned my gun against the tree, hung my hunting bag on its branch, and sat at its foot.

Having rested for a while, I stood up, gathered some dry sticks together, and made a fire with them. Then I roasted four of the coco-yams that were in my hunting bag. I prefer carrying coco-yams with me in the bush because coco-yams do not spoil for many days. Having roasted those coco-yams, I ate them. Then I took my tobacco pipe from my bag and started smoking at the foot of this tree. Having enjoyed my pipe, I lit my hunting lamp and hung it on my hunting cap. Animals would not run away once they saw this light; they would simply fasten their eyes on it until a hunter fired at them. I put the cap on my head and saw clearly by the light attached to it.

Though tigers, lions, elephants, deers, boas, and apes were common in this bush, I travelled far before I could get a small animal. With reluctance I fired at this small animal and killed it. I brought it back to that small tree, roasted it and ate most of it. It was fat and very sweet, though it was small.

Since the distance from this bush to my town was great, and since I was tired, I cut many palm-tree leaves and laid them on the ground, one upon another. Then I lay on them, putting my gun on my right side and my hunting bag on my left side, and I was soon fast asleep. But what prevented me from enjoying my sleep for many hours was my fear of snakes and scorpions, which I knew to be numerous everywhere in this bush. Remembering that these pests were very dangerous and could hurt me, I stood up, took my gun and bag, and climbed that small tree to the top. I hardly sat on its branches before I was fast asleep.

However, what frightened me even more was that when I woke up, I discovered that this small tree had carried me a distance of about five miles. Terrified, I thought of jumping down, but it occurred to me that if I jumped down, the bad spirit living inside this tree would harm me. So this tree continued to carry me deeply into the bush until I saw clearly that it was carrying me straight to the Bush of Ghosts. I started to struggle to jump down but found that I was tied to the tree's branches. I tried to take my spells and charms from my hunting bag, but my hand could not reach the bag. Had I been able to use one of my spells or charms, I would have succeeded in escaping from the tree. But in the end, this small tree carried me into the Bush of Ghosts by force.

All my efforts had failed and I began to despair. I cried out, "This is the first time I have gone to hunt in the bush after my father's death, and this is the first time I have had such a bad experience. How can I escape from all the ghosts living in the bush to which this small tree is carrying me?" Thus was I despairing as the tree carried me further and further into the bush.

I was panic-stricken because my father had told me fearful news of this bush before he died. He had said that since the creation of the world no human being had ever entered this bush either by intention or by mistake and returned home. This bush and its ghostly inhabitants were so bad that if an animal chased by a hunter managed to reach it, then the animal was safe, for the hunter would turn back and go away rather than enter into this bush.

Ah, my friends -- males, females and children -- who read this book, I tell you now that one who travels far and wide will definitely see many strange things that are beyond the realm of human thought. But he will also suffer greatly and perhaps even die on his travels unless God saves his life!

I cannot describe in full all the bad things that existed in this perilous bush. It happened to be on the way to heaven so everyone who died on earth travelled through it when going to heaven. Those who were bad turned into ghosts and remained there while others who were good passed through it peacefully on their way to heaven. This bush was the dwelling place of Satan, who was driven away from heaven by God. It also was home to ghosts with seven heads, sixteen heads, etc. Many different towns of ghosts were there so the languages spoken by the ghosts differed from place to place also.

As soon as I arrived at the center of this perilous bush, I fell off my small tree in front of one mighty tree, but instead of hitting the ground, I remained hanging in the air. My feet did not touch the ground, and my hands did not touch anything. The air that held me up was thick. After a while I found myself on the ground in front of the mighty tree but I could not move my body. The circumference of this tree was about 140 feet and its height was about 900 feet. To add to my fear, the tree which brought me there suddenly turned to a fearful ghost in my presence. My fears were increased when I saw him knocking at the mighty tree as one knocks at the door of a house. After a while a part of the mighty tree opened and a ghost peeped out. I saw clearly that the head of that ghost was just like that of a cow with horns. When he looked at me and I looked fearfully at him, my eyes were nearly blinded by a strange light that penetrated me from his powerful eyes. Having looked at me sternly for some minutes, he and the ghost who had changed from the small tree entered into that mighty tree. Then the open part of that tree was closed.

Fifteen minutes later the tree opened again like a big door, and these two ghosts came out. One had a thick rope in his hand. They told me to surrender my gun and hunting bag to them, and when I gave both of these things to them, they pushed me to another tree about fifty yards away. They tied me so tightly to that tree with their rope that I could hardly breathe in and out. Then they put my gun and bag by my side and returned into the tree, slamming the heavy door behind them. Thus they left me there to my fate.

But to my surprise, after a few minutes I heard the sound of drums and the noise of merriments as if an important festival of 'Egungun' was being performed in a very big town. Of course, the inside of this tree was a big town for the ghosts of that area. The noises were so great that I heard them clearly. At the same time I heard the cry of birds, so I knew that it was three o'clock in the morning. I could tell the time of the day or night by the cries of birds, especially doves.

After a while six ghosts came out. They loosened

the rope from my body and dragged me with force into the tree. It was then that I saw clearly that all the buildings were beautiful but the ghostly inhabitants were very dirty and were smelling just like decaying dead bodies. Many of them had no eyes. Those with eyes had no mouth, those with heads had no caps, those with caps had no heads on which to put their caps, and many had no ears at all. As they were walking about sluggishly, they were nearly trampling many of their creeping little children to death. It was as if they were doing everything foolishly.

When they dragged me to their king, they presented me to him as an animal and told him to sacrifice me for their festival which was in seven days' time. But their king was very pleased with me as a gift and he thanked them greatly. He prayed earnestly that the creator would continue to assist them to get animals like me for him whenever their festival was approaching. "Let it be so," all of them shouted.

I now wondered how I could avoid this death. For instance, though I had many spells and charms which had power to save me from these ghosts, I could not use them because everything seemed like a dream and I could not decide what to do. It seemed to me that I could not survive, for I had no chance to escape from this town. I was bitterly hungry, but there was no food for me to eat because all of the foods eaten by these ghosts were not cooked. Moreover, only two days remained before their festival. I was praying earnestly to God to spare me from this death but I did not know how this could be done. "But how can I save myself? Please, tell me!" I lamented to myself.

All the clothes used by the king were kept in the garden in which they put me. When only one day remained before they were to kill me, the whole palace was to be cleaned by these ghosts. I knew that the ghosts were going to wash this heap of clothes in the river that morning, so in the dark of the night, when I was sure that none of these ghosts were near there, I hid inside one of the heaps of clothes. I squatted in there without making any motion.

At five o'clock in the morning many ghosts entered the garden and carried the bundles of clothes, with me inside, to their river, far away from their town. There they put the bundles down on a riverbank without knowing that I was hidden inside one. Then they left everything there and went to greet their friends who were some distance away on the same riverbank. It was on that day that I learned that ghosts greeted one another.

As soon as they had walked a few yards away, I came out of the bundle of clothes cautiously. Then, without hesitation, I ran away before they returned. That was how God saved me from these ghosts. Fearlessly, I went back to the tree to which they had tied me before taking me inside the tree for killing. I grabbed my gun and hunting bag and ran to another part of the bush.

There were five different towns in this Bush of the Ghosts. Ghosts, those dead people who were bad before they died and also those whom God drove out of heaven, were living in these five towns.

As I was roaming about, trying to find the right way to my town, I met another ghost unexpectedly. He was terrible and carried a fire with big flames on his head. The fire was so big that almost every part of the bush was as bright as daytime when he stood up high. On meeting him, I took to my heels at once, but

I had not run more than ten yards when he shouted at me to stop. Since each of his arms was about twenty feet long and could reach the topmost of any tree, he did not have to chase me far before stretching out his hands and holding me powerless. When he stopped me, I noticed that his nose was almost three feet long and very wide. He was terribly stout, and I knew his name was "Fear." My father had told me about the bad behavior of this ghost.

As he approached me, he asked whether I was a human being or a spirit. I was frightened when I heard this question from him. Before replying, I hesitated in great confusion, and it was then that I saw that he was not more than two feet tall, although the big fire he carried made him seem much taller. I finally replied that I was a human being but that I did not belong among the people who were in heaven. He then asked for what purpose I had come to their town, or did I not know that people from earth were forbidden to come to their town? Did I not know that any earthly people who dared come there would perish or perhaps be turned into ghosts? I was very embarrassed and fearful when I heard this. Again I lamented to myself that it now seemed certain that I would never return to my town.

To make things worse, he demanded that I should take the fire from his head, put it on my head, and keep on going along with him. When I heard this, I started to run away with fear, but he chased me immediately and caught me within a few seconds. To my surprise, the fire on his head did not fall off at all while he was doing this. When he gripped me, his long hand was so hot that my body was nearly burnt into ashes. I shouted, "Ah, I fear your fire! I cannot carry it because I have never carried fire in my life!"

But he continued to insist that I carry his fire. When I refused stubbornly, he grew annoyed. I tried to get one of my spells ready, but he suddenly snatched both my gun and hunting bag, threw them to one side, and then started to beat me. In pain, I started to beat him in return. After a while our mutual beating turned into a fight. Our fight gradually became so terrible that all the animals around us fled far away from that area. All the birds kept quiet inside their nests, and even the breeze stopped blowing. The whole bush remained silent. But as our fight became fiercer, many ghosts of his kind came out to watch us. Each time he tried to knock me down, he failed, but I couldn't knock him down either. We wrestled for over two hours, and because I was so tired, I nearly fainted. Finally I ran to my gun, picked it up, pointed it at him, and pulled the trigger, but my gun failed to fire. Instead, only water came out of it. Now I was totally depressed.

To prove to me that ghosts had more power than people, he took the gun from me and drank the water that was coming out of it. On seeing him do so, I became more depressed. However, I still maintained my hope. I ran to my cutlass, seized it, and with all my power tried to cut his shoulder with it. But the cutlass simply broke into two. He did not even feel a slight pain in his shoulder. Having seen this, I lost hope of safety at once and lamented loudly that "This ghost will kill me today!"

He was aware that I was tired out and depressed, so he told me to sit down and rest. Then he picked up my broken cutlass, put both pieces into the big fire on his head, joined them together, and threw my cutlass back to me. Feeling that I had rested enough, he told me to stand up. But when I stood up wearily, what I did first was to pick up my cutlass. Then I hung my bag on my shoulder and held my gun.

When he saw that I had collected everything, he told me to bend over. I knew that my gun, cutlass and spells had no effect on him, so I lowered my back and he jumped on it and started to ride me around the bush like a horse. If I tired or slowed down, he was so wicked that he did not allow me to rest even for one second, but he flogged me instead. He continued to ride me this way till it was nearly dawn.

At dawn he rode me to his house. When he dismounted from my back in front of his house, he put a rope around my neck and tied it to a tree. He also put a saddle on my back so I would be ready for another riding. Then he went inside. A few minutes later his wife brought me a large quantity of grass. She put it in front of me, nearly touching my mouth. I looked at the grass sorrowfully for a few minutes and began to shed tears.

After a while the ghost came out and rode me to his friend's house. On reaching there, he fastened me to a tree near the house. After he entered the house, all the ghosts of that area came to me. They surrounded me, looking at me with surprise for I was strange to them.

Some minutes later the ghost (my captor) and his friend came out to see me. His friend touched every part of my body and was surprised that I could carry my captor wherever he wanted to go. In his presence my captor jumped on my back and rode me back to the nearby house. By this time a stable had already been built for me. Then I was dragged into it, and a strong rope was fastened to my neck and tied to a wooden pillar. But this stable was so small that I was unable to stand upright or to move here and there so I remained always on my knees. An hour later my captor's boy brought me some bananas with water. Since I was bitterly hungry, I started to eat the raw bananas. But while I was doing this sorrowfully, the small boy jumped on my back and tried to ride me while the rope was still on my neck. He prevented me from eating the raw bananas, and when I tasted the water he brought, I discovered there was a lot of salt in it.

This boy had hardly gone away when the friend of

my captor came in. He had asked to borrow me, for he wanted to go to a place about twelve miles away. My captor was pleased to release me to him, and without mercy, the friend jumped on my back. As he was riding me along, many ghost children began to shout at me happily for they were glad to have something like me to ride about.

What surprised me most in this town of ghosts was that every important ghost there carried fire with big flames on his head. This one who rode me now also carried fire on his head. He rode me for five hours before reaching his destination. Then he tied me to a pillar in the sun in front of a house where a marriage ceremony was taking place. The sun scorched me and I was perspiring continuously. Many ghosts in this town came out and looked at me with astonishment. All of them were amazed to see that an earthly man could be ridden about. This was strange to them because they had no horses at all in any of the towns of ghosts, and they did not even know what a horse was called.

Ah, but these ghosts were very wicked. For instance, when the bride and the bridegroom were ready to go to the church for their marriage service, both of them mounted on my back without checking to see if my backbone would break under their weight, and they rode me back again after the service. When they returned, they tied me to the same spot. Luckily they gave me food after a while, but it was remnants of rice and many other useless kinds of food that the ghosts had rejected. They gave me water too, but it was very sour. However, I drank it like that because I was thirsty and there was nothing else to quench my thirst.

To my surprise, I saw that the reverend in their church was the Devil himself. The place I call a church was an assembly place for all the ghosts. After the marriage ceremony had ended on the third day, that ghost who was a friend of my captor put all the drinks which were given to him on my back and mounted me. As he was riding me along on the road, he met the aunt of my captor five miles from his destination, and the aunt mounted me as well. They were much too heavy for me to carry. He wanted me to walk fast but I could not. He began to flog me till every part of my body was bloody, and he continued riding me to my captor's house. When we finally arrived at five o'clock in the evening, my captor told his boy to drag me to the small stable.

This boy started to ill-treat me as he dragged me into my stable.

Later, when the ghosts of this town realized that I could be of use to them too, they all started to borrow me from my captor for riding on journeys. However, he gave me to them on hire instead of free of charge. Now I had no time to rest at all, and after a while I became lean. One day, when I counted up the number of years that I had been captured, I saw that it had been three years and I started to plan how to escape from my captor.

One morning I lay down flat without breathing, and pretended to be dead. When the boy came into the stable and saw how I lay breathless, he removed the rope from my neck and examined every part of my body. Still I did not breathe. He ran to my captor, who was his father, but this ghost was taking his bath at that time. After the bath the boy told his father that I was dead, but before they came to the stable, I had taken my gun and hunting bag and run far away. That was how I escaped from this ghost who was called "Fear." Even though "Fear" was so strong that my gun, cutlass, spells, and charms had no effect on him, God

Almighty saved me from him in the end, and I thanked
Him for that.

The Second Town of the Ghosts

One night, as I was still struggling to find the way to my town, I saw a ghost called Hunger coming toward me. When I looked at him closely, I saw that he was very stout and holding a small mat about two feet long. He himself was terrible in appearance and his head was tapered like a top. As soon as I saw that he was coming toward me, I started to run away for my life. He did not chase me more than forty yards when he overtook me. He held me and immediately started to drag me to his town, the second town of the ghosts. I began to lament loudly, "Ah, I have fallen into the hands of a ghost. I have started another punishment!"

This second town of the ghosts was underground. The sun could not shine on it, so it was dark both day and night. Furthermore, all the ghosts living in this town were unable to go anywhere in daylight. Once there was light, they were powerless. They had no food and water there, and I saw that whenever one of them got sick, the others killed him and ate him at once.

They were the most wicked of the ghosts. For this, God hated them so much that He did not provide for their needs.

When the ghost called Hunger had nearly dragged me to this town, he put his forefinger on my eyes. To my horror, as soon as he did so, both my eyes went blind. When I could not see at all, he dragged me into the town and then to his house and pushed me into one of his rooms. While I squatted inside the room, I began to lament in whispers, "Ah, I have become a blind man! There is no way for me to return to my hometown anymore. Even when I was not blind I could not find the road to my hometown, so how will I be able to find it now that I have become blind? I am sure now that I shall never return to my town."

I did not know that as I was lamenting like this, the ghost whose name was Hunger and several others were busy preparing a big fire inside a huge pit. When the fire was ready, Hunger sent one of his men to come and escort me to him. He and his fellow ghosts wanted to roast me in that fire and eat me. When the escort entered the room, he pushed me out and told me to follow him. I did so, but he wanted me to walk quickly, and I could not for I was blind. He put his left forefinger on my eyes just as Hunger had done. To my surprise, he had hardly done so when I regained my eyesight. I was extremely happy when my eyes were as they had been before, although I was still a captive they were preparing to eat soon.

I continued to follow that fellow, but as I followed him, I had enough time to take one of my spells out of my hunting bag and to put my gun on my left shoulder. The miraculous power of that spell was that if it was thrown onto the ground, it would change night into day at once. So without hesitation I threw this spell onto the ground unexpectedly, and there was light immediately. Since the escort could not see or move now, I ran off to the main gate of the town.

There I asked the gateman to allow me to pass out to the bush, but he refused because he knew that if I escaped, there would be nothing for the ghosts to eat that day. I insisted on leaving, but he held me tightly, so I threw my spell onto the ground and night changed into day immediately. However, I did not know that this gateman also had similar spells with him. In fact, he had two that could be used to change day into night. But my own were four in number. Having seen that I had changed night into day, he threw one of his own onto the ground and it turned day into night immediately. Then he dragged me back inside the gate. But I hastily threw another one of my spells onto the ground and night again turned into day, this time with a hot sun. He did not waste time but he threw the last one that he had onto the ground, and day became night. Now he had no more spells left, but I still had two and they were specially made for changing anything into another object. When I saw Hunger and his fellows coming to catch me at this gate, I snatched myself from the gateman and threw another spell onto the ground so that they and their town caught fire suddenly. When I saw that all of them had perished, I left there gladly.

Three days later I was still looking for the road to my town, and I saw a woman far away. She had two heads, one facing her front, and the other facing her back. Under each of her arms she had three breasts. She looked even more fearful than the ghosts I had seen in the past, so I took to my heels. Even though she was a two-headed woman, she started to chase me about in this bush. As she ran, her six breasts were beating her body, sounding like people beating water with their palms.

As I was running away from this woman, I saw a very narrow path. I followed it but she continued to chase me fiercely. After a while I came to a sharp corner, and on rounding this corner, I met another ghost unexpectedly. He was short and stout and had two horns on his head, each of them curved outward. This ghost was terrible indeed. Anyone meeting him suddenly, would nearly faint at his dreadful appearance. He stood firmly in the center of the path and stretched out both his arms, one to the left and the other to the right. In his right hand he was holding the head of a human being. What made me so afraid was that the head was twitching and resembled the head of a man whom I knew very well in my town. However, this head had two wings. The ghost, who continued to eat the head greedily, also held a horrible small mat woven with the bones of human beings. This ghost no sooner saw me than I heard him thank his creator for providing something for him to eat that night. It was about six o'clock p.m. when he said that. He kept looking at me terribly.

Then the two-headed woman who chased me around that sharp corner arrived. She stood at my back while the other one stood in front of me, blocking my way. The short, stout one shouted that I should follow him to the place where he would kill me for dinner. But the two-headed ghostess who stood behind me shouted, "No! It is not you he will follow but me because I was the very one who chased this earthly person to this corner!" The ghost who blocked my way replied, "No! This earthly person is my food tonight. I shall take him to the place where I shall kill and eat him!" Both of them shouted angrily at each other for a few minutes, and then they started to fight. Since my gun was useless against ghosts, I just left them there and began to run away for my life.

Soon I came to a huge hole not far from that corner. Without hesitation I entered this huge hole with my useless gun and hunting bag and hid myself in there. When the two-headed ghostess and the short ghost saw that I had run away, they stopped their fight and started to hunt for me. Unfortunately, I did not know that the huge hole in which I had hidden myself belonged to a fretful ghost who was also in the hole at that time. As the other two were hunting for me, they were shouting horribly, letting the other ghosts know that a human being had just escaped from them. On hearing their shouts, all the ghosts in that area rushed out to them.

The fretful ghost heard their shout also, and as he was going out to them, he saw me in his hole. Instead of having mercy on me, he began to push me out, shouting, "This is the man! This is the earthly person that you are looking for!" Without hesitation the two fighters and the others rushed into his hole, and all of them dragged me out by force.

It was then that I noticed that this fretful ghost in whose hole I hid myself had two horns on his head as well. All his teeth were about five inches long and stuck out of his mouth. His upper and lower lips were unable to cover these teeth which were as sharp as a big saw used for cutting logs of wood. All of them were as brown as brown polish. His legs swelled out like those of a stuffed doll, and his thighs held his stomach up. Though this ghost was very kind, he was fretful, ugly, and had many fingers which were not equal.

Having dragged me out of the hole, they started to ask me a number of questions: "Where do you come from?" I replied that I had come from earth. "What do you come here for?" I explained that I was brought to their bush by a tree on top of which I slept when I was hunting near my town. They said, "Yes, the ghosts of the first town of ghosts had reported to us that you had run away from them!" Then they took me to the palace of their king, who told them that they should prepare to sacrifice me to their gods.

When their king said that, the two-headed ghostess who was first chasing me about stood up. She told the king that she wanted to marry me and that was why she was chasing me about. But their king would not agree to this. The fretful ghost in whose hole I had hidden myself stood up and shouted that he supported the two-headed ghostess. I did not know that this fretful ghost was the father of the two-headed ghostess. However, when he insisted that he supported the two-headed ghostess's plan to marry me, the king agreed. Meanwhile the ghost who blocked my way when the two-headed ghostess was chasing me stood up. He said that he was the ghost who stopped me when I was running away and therefore he had the right to kill me for his dinner because he had no other food to eat that night. At this stage the king reminded him that the two-headed ghostess was the first to chase me. But the short ghost stood up again and told the king that he was the one who blocked my way and stopped me; otherwise I would have escaped from them. The fretful ghost replied that if he had not found me in his hole, nobody would have found me. Again the ghost who stopped me stood up and suggested that the king should cut me into two equal halves so he could take one half as his own share and have something to eat that night.

This ghost had hardly finished saying that when he began to scrape my body with his thick tongue, which was as sharp as sandpaper. Within a few minutes every part of my body was bleeding as if somebody had dragged me on rough ground. This ghost was so greedy for food that he could not go for even a second without eating something. He ate from morning till night and from night till morning. Even in the presence of all the other ghosts he started to eat the log of wood on which they all sat in the palace and he nearly finished it in a few minutes. I was looking at him that night with only half an eye, but I noticed that he ate more than a cooking pot. So when he insisted that their king should cut me into two and give him his own share because he was terribly hungry for food, the fretful ghost stood up again and told him that he would give him a different thing to eat that night. Fortunately, when the short ghost heard so, he agreed.

After this hot argument, all of us left the palace, following the fretful ghost and his daughter (the two-headed ghostess) to his hole. Then her father begged me to marry his daughter. He explained to me that if I married his daughter, I would continue living with them until I turned into a ghost. But this made me greatly afraid. I asked myself how I could marry a woman with two heads and six breasts. Instead of agreeing, I started to think of how I could escape from them. Meanwhile he continued to explain to me that if I married his daughter, I would turn into one of them after thirty years and then I would never die. However, I was so frightened that I did not follow his advice. Having completed two months in this huge hole with these ghosts, I still wanted to go back to my town. One day, after they had gone to their meeting place at ten o'clock at night, I took my gun and hunting bag and went away from that hole immediately. That was how I left the ghost who wanted to eat me and how I also escaped from the two-headed ghostess who wanted to marry me by force.

The Third Town of the Ghosts

When I left the Second Town of the Ghosts without much harm or punishment, I thanked God greatly. Then I repaired my gun and began to roam about, looking for the way to my town. I was anxious to return home because these ghosts were troubling me so much that I never had any rest. I was fed up with them.

I was still searching when I saw a ghost sitting on top of a stone under the shade of a tree. This ghost had four heads, four mouths and four horse-like tails. On each of his four heads he had four eyes and four ears. Although the ears resembled those of a horse, they were bigger. His eyes and mouths were also abnormally large. When I met him there, a snake was lying beside him. The head of this snake was just like the head of a big bird, though curved like the handle of a walking stick and almost covered with short feathers. The rest of its body was like that of the snake.

As soon as I met this strange snake, I wanted to fire my gun at it, but the four-headed ghost raised his heads up suddenly and said in a sorrowful voice, "Please, earthly person, do not kill my snake, because it is my messenger and is providing all my needs. If you kill it, I will soon die of hunger, so do not kill it, please." After the ghost told me this, I stopped aiming at the snake, and the ghost started to tell me his own story. "Do you see me as I am? The God who created me gave me this form because when I was in heaven, I was very wicked and used to trouble His angels. As time went on, my wickedness got worse, so he sent me to the Devil, the king of hell, in the fifth town of the ghosts, telling him to punish me in the fires of hell for twenty-five years. God did this so I might repent. But after I had spent twenty-five years in the fires of hell, the Devil sent me back to God, saying my wickedness had tripled. God returned me to the Devil so I could roast in hellfires for forty years more. I spent that period with pleasure in hell, but my wickedness only increased further. When God saw this, He cursed me, declaring, 'Now I drive you away from heaven to the Bush of the Ghosts, where you are to remain among wild beasts, poisonous snakes and scorpions.' Since that day, I have found myself in this Bush of the Ghosts where I have been bitten by wild beasts and snakes and stung by scorpions and ants. When God told me that He was condemning me to various punishments forever, I made it clear to Him that I would never change my bad character." Thus this ghost related to me the story of his stubborn defiance of God.

As he was telling me all this earnestly with his four mouths, these mouths were arguing with one another and sounding like big bells. They were making noise like one hundred persons talking, and their eyes were turning round and round.

After hearing his story to the end, I became sad and felt sorry for him. But when I advised him to change his bad character so God Almighty could have mercy on him and take the punishment away from him, he simply replied immediately that he would not change it at all. He told me further that he was waiting for even more punishments from God. Having heard so from this stubborn ghost, I sighed heavily.

I took my water bottle out of my hunting bag and

drank, for I had been in the sun all the while he was telling me his story, and I was thirsty. It had taken him two hours and fifteen minutes to tell me his story. As I was preparing to put the water bottle back into my hunting bag, he begged me to offer him some of the water to quench his thirst. He also told me with a sad voice that throughout the sixty-five years that he had spent in the fires of hell and even since he had come out, he had not tasted even a drop of water. When he finished this sorrowful story, I told him with great sadness to raise his four mouths up and to open them. I wanted to pour the water into one of the mouths, but every one of them was struggling to quench its thirst first. I looked at all of them with embarrassment for a few minutes and then simply started to pour the water into the mouth on the left side of the head of this stubborn ghost. But this mouth had hardly swallowed two drops of the water when this ghost and his snake suddenly turned into a little hill near the way to heaven. I immediately wrote his name, which was called "WOE," on the hill for the rest of the bad ghosts to see whenever they passed through there. Then I left that place and continued searching for the way to my town.

As I continued to wander about in this jungle of ghosts, I saw an old woman sitting in front of a fire on the bank of a big river. I greeted her and she replied. Then I begged her to let me light my pipe with her fire and she agreed. Soon after I lit my pipe, I bade her goodbye, but as I was going away, she called me back and asked me what I had in my bag. When I told her that I had only a small yam, she asked me for it, and I gave it to her. She was very happy to receive this small yam, and after thanking me well, she put her hand into the fire and brought a spirit spell out from it. The very small spell was inside an antelope horn. When she gave it to me, she told me that whenever I met a ghost who wanted to kill me, I should swallow it, for it would turn me into a ram with horns on its head. After hearing her explanation of the uses of the spell, I took it from her and thanked her. Then I went on my way. It was later that I found out that this old woman was the spirit of that river.

After leaving her, I travelled for three days. I was getting tired and worried about roaming about, so when I saw a tree, I stopped under it and put my gun and hunting bag down. I rested there for three months and thirteen days exactly. Having regained my strength, I then continued my journey to the northeast of this third Bush of the Ghosts, following a narrow stream which was flowing to the north. The trees lining both banks of the stream almost covered it, and I found fifteen calabashes along my way.

The water of the stream was as cold as ice. When I came to a narrow road crossing over the stream, I was glad, for I thought that this was the road to my town. Happily I put my gun and hunting bag down on the bank, took off my clothes, and entered the stream. I bathed to my satisfaction, because ever since getting lost in this bush six years before, I had never bathed even once. After my bath, I drank some water and got dressed.

Then I remembered that there was no more water in my water bottle, so I took one of the calabashes and filled it from the stream. As soon as I started to throw water into my bottle, I saw that every part of this stream began to shake as if it wanted to swallow me. I raised my head up with fright, and this time I saw sixteen ghosts following one another and coming to cross the stream. Unfortunately, they were on the very road that I suspected to be the road to my town. They marched in single file, and I noticed that the ghost who was in front had one head, the second ghost had two, the third had three, and each of the rest had as many heads as the number that he was in line. Their leader had sixteen heads. As soon as the ghost with one head reached the stream and saw me there, he asked me to give him water to drink. Fearfully I picked up one of the fifteen calabashes, filled it with water and gave it to him. But instead of drinking the water and returning the calabash, he opened his mouth and swallowed the calabash as well as the water that was inside it. Then he told me to get ready to serve water to the two-headed ghost who was coming behind him, and he crossed the stream and disappeared.

I was puzzled and frightened when I saw this ghost swallow the calabash as well as the water, and I was still thinking about this when the two-headed ghost arrived and asked me to serve him water. With fear and confusion I took another one of the fifteen calabashes, filled it up with water and gave it to him. To my surprise, he too swallowed both the water and the calabash just as the first one had done. He then told me to prepare to serve water to the three-headed ghost who was coming behind him. It was like that with each of these ghosts: each swallowed the water along with the calabash and went away.

I was in a state of fear and confusion when their leader, who had sixteen heads on his huge neck, arrived. I began to tremble when I looked at him with half an eye and saw that on each of his heads there was a town in which many kinds of creatures lived. Each town had a fire, tall trees, and rivers with big canoes moving about. Several wild beasts lived there as well. When I looked more closely, I saw that poisonous creatures such as snakes, scorpions, ants, etc., were living on all of his sixteen heads too. Both his palms were very hot. As I stood sweating terribly as if I was in a foundry or big boiler, he shouted at me to give him water. With extreme fear I looked up and down, wondering where to get the calabash with which to take water from the stream. The fifteen ghosts who had preceded him had swallowed all fifteen of the calabashes. But at last, thinking that he could not swallow me, I joined my palms together, filled them with water, and stretched them to him so he could drink water from them. But to my horror this sixteen-headed ghost swallowed me up with the water. As soon as he had done this, he crossed the stream and followed the fifteen others who had preceded him to a place about fifty miles away.

As he was carrying me along, I sat down in his stomach and began to think. Perhaps I could cut a hole in his stomach with my cutlass and then escape through it. But when I tried this with all my power, I was unable to cut into his stomach at all, and he did not feel even the smallest pain. Seeing that my cutlass could not do anything to him, I tried to fire my gun at his stomach but it failed to fire because it was already wet. Then I lit a match to burn his stomach, hoping that when the fire forced him to pass excrement, I might come out with it. But the fire did nothing to him.

After a while I remembered the spell that the old woman sitting by the fire near the big river had given me when I had offered her a piece of yam. The spell transformed a person into a ram with horns on its head. When the sixteen-headed ghost stopped and started to excrete, I swallowed the spell and it turned me to this kind of big ram. I suddenly came out along with his excrement, but as soon as he saw me on the ground, he pounced on me, wanting to swallow me again. However, he failed because I started to run away immediately, and when he chased me, his heads began to get entangled in big trees, small trees and running plants. He ran as fast as he could to catch me, but all those things obstructed his way. At last, when he saw that he could not run as fast as he wanted to, he left me and went back to his fellow ghosts.

I continued running away but ran unexpectedly into a tiger. He started to chase me immediately for he wanted to kill and eat me, so I kept on running desperately. Then I fell into the hands of sheep rearers who caught me by putting a rope around my neck. They put me among their sheep because they thought that I was a real ram. I tried to change to my usual form but I failed. I then realized that I had forgotten to ask the old woman what I should do to change back into a man. These sheep rearers drove me and the flock of sheep to their town. When it was dawn, they took us to a market to be sold. This was eight miles away, and when we arrived there, they tied us all to a big tree in the center of that market. Three hours later they brought us some grass to eat. The real rams rushed to the grass happily and began to eat it greedily. I alone was unable to eat it for I was not really a ram.

When the rearers noticed that I did not eat the grass, they pushed me toward the other rams so I could share the grass with them, but I still refused to eat it. After a while their customers came and bought many of us, but I was not among those chosen. At exactly three o'clock the sheep rearers took the rest of us back to their town. The following morning they took us to another market fifteen miles away, and after some hours their customers came and bought some of us. When the sheep rearers noticed that their customers would not even touch me, they tried to call attention to me, but their customers complained that I was too lean. At four o'clock the sheep rearers drove us back to their town and kept us in their yard as usual. They brought some corn, and I rushed to it with the other rams, but as I struggled to eat it, the other rams interfered. The sheep rearers just stood and watched us.

The next day there was no market so they drove us to a field and loosened the ropes on our necks so we could eat the grass. The other rams were going from one place to another, eating the grass greedily, but I stood in one spot and did not eat. Noticing this, the sheep rearers decided that if they took me to the market once more and their customers still refused to buy me, they would kill me on that very day. Of course, I overheard their decision, but I could not turn myself back into a person to show them I was not a ram. I continued to wrap myself in sorrow until the next market day arrived.

Again their customers bought many of us but refused to buy me. When the market closed for the day and they were taking us back to town, the sheep rearers began to tell one another that I had bad luck. When we got to their town, they drove us into the yard as usual and brought some remnants of food for us to eat. They saw that I ate these remnants along with the other rams, so they changed their minds about killing me. The next morning they drove us to another marketplace and tied us to another big tree. Their customers arrived and bought ten of us but refused totally to buy me, saying that I was too lean. This time the sheep rearers reduced my price to seven shillings and six pence, yet their customers continued to refuse to buy me. They tried as hard as they could to sell me but it was all in vain. When the market closed for that day, they drove those of us who were unsold back to their house, saying angrily that if they took me to the market the following morning and no one bought me, they would surely kill me. As I lay on the ground in the yard thinking that the sheep rearers were about to kill me, the rest of the rams began to kick me, jump on me and make noises so that I was unable to sleep.

After three months and four days in the hands of these shepherds, I was taken the following morning to a town. Their customers arrived and bought many of us but they did not buy me. As soon as they left, a woman came to the market at ten o'clock and offered seven shillings and six pence for me. The sheep rearers were very glad to sell me to the woman for that price, and I was very glad the woman bought me. After having put a thick rope around my neck, she dragged me home and tied me to a tree in front of her house. It was the rainy season, and she left me out in the rain, so I was feeling very cold.

I did not know that the son of this woman had been

drowned in the very river on the bank of which I had met the old woman who had given me the spell for turning myself into a ram. It was this old woman (actually the spirit of the river) who held the son of the woman who had just bought me. When she had learned that her son was being held by the spirit of the river (the old woman), she wanted to know how to get her son back, so she went to a man who was a future-teller. The future-teller explained to her that if she wanted the spirit of the river to release her son, she would have to buy a ram and tie it onto a tree near the river. Then in the night the spirit would come out of the river, take the ram away, and leave the son there. After I had spent three days in front of this woman's house, she took me to the river, tied me onto a nearby tree, and left me there alone. I remained at the foot of that tree for seven days without eating or drinking. The rains and the sun were beating me there.

On midnight of the seventh day I saw the old woman (spirit of the river) coming out of that river, holding a boy. Having come out completely, she started to come straight toward me. I was so frightened that I fainted three times before she and the boy reached me. I did not know that she was the same old woman (spirit of the river) who had given me the spell which had changed me into a ram. She loosened the rope that was around my neck, left the boy at the foot of the tree, and then took me to the bottom of the river. That was how the boy was saved.

I was surprised that my body did not get wet at all when she took me to the bottom of the river. To my astonishment, the bottom of this river was a big town, and all the houses there were built entirely with glass. When she took me to her own house, she put me in her parlor which was glass as well. When I entered the parlor, I saw myself reflected in the glass in the form of a ram with horns. Suddenly I turned back into a man with my gun and hunting bag on my shoulder. Then she told me to sit down, and she brought food to me -- the same kind of food that was eaten in my town. I ate to my satisfaction, having never tasted this nice kind of food since when I had entered this Bush of the Ghosts.

Within ten minutes I had finished everything, and she returned to her parlor and began to ask me questions. "Do you know me?" she asked. I replied,

"I do." Then she asked, "Where do you know me from?" I explained to her that one day, when I was passing near a big river, I saw her sitting on the river bank and I begged her to allow me to light my pipe from the fire which she had made in front of her. She in turn begged me to give her a small yam and then offered me a spell that turned me into a ram when I swallowed it. She then said to me that if I had not given her the small yam on that day, she would have killed me now, turned me into a spirit, or given me to one of the gods they worshipped under that river.

After ten hours of conversation in that house, she told me to stand up and follow her. Then she began to show me every part of that town. She showed me the gods they were worshipping there, but as we were going around the town, I noticed that there was not a single church. When I asked her why there was no church in their beautiful town, she asked me to explain what a church was. I said that a church was a place where the God who created us was worshipped. To my surprise, she replied that they did not know this God because none of them had died since they had arrived in that town and they would never die, or so she said to me.

After some hours we returned to her house, and it was then that I told her the story of the spell she offered me when I met her sitting on the bank of the river. I told her that I had hardly swallowed the spell when it had turned me into a ram with two long horns on its head. However, when I had wanted to return to my former self and be a hunter again, I had not known how to do it. That was when I knew that I had made a great mistake by not asking how to reverse the spell. When she heard this, she asked me to give the spell back to her and I did so. Instead of returning it to me, she gave me nine grains of alligator pepper -- another kind of a spell -- and explained that whenever I met a ghost or any other kind of harmful creature who wanted to kill or punish me, I should use these grains, for they would turn me into a big bird or rain or something else so that I would be safe. She told me further that it would not be hard for me to change myself back to my natural form. I took the nine grains from her and thanked her.

Advising me to take my gun and hunting bag, she then gave me a mirror and told me to look at it. To my surprise, no sooner had I looked at the mirror than I found myself back in the Bush of the Ghosts.

The Fourth Town of the Ghosts

Having found myself in the Bush of the Ghosts again, I began to roam about in it once more. When I got tired, I saw a log of wood and sat on it, thinking about this dreadful bush. I realized that these ghosts could no longer harm me for the spirit of the river had offered me her juju grains, so I left the log and continued to walk about in the bush. But I had not done so for more than two hours when I saw an orange tree far away from me. I started to go to the tree anxiously, but before I reached it, I saw a strange creature who was plucking oranges from it. In fact, he was swallowing them greedily as soon as they fell on the ground. This creature was half crocodile and half man, and I prepared to fire at him immediately. Before I could do so, he started to come toward me, and I saw then that one of his eyes was like brass, his left arm was like lead, while his right foot was just like copper metal. When this crocodile-man saw that I held a gun, he hastily turned himself into fire and started running toward me. I took one of the nine grains of alligator pepper, and it turned me into a heavy rain which quenched that fire at once. Then this crocodile-man turned into a big snake about fourteen feet long and about seven feet in diameter. Just as he was preparing to swallow me, I hastily turned into a long, thick stick and began to beat him hard. But when the snake was nearly beaten to death, it turned into a big tree. Then I hastily turned the stick into an ax and it started to fell the tree. Just when this tree was about to fall down, it changed into a very thick smoke and covered the ax so that I could hardly breathe. But then I too hastily changed into a strong breeze and blew the smoke far away. Having blown back to the spot where our fight had started, I changed from the breeze into a hunter, my former form, and continued to walk along in this bush.

It was not long before I saw a young ghost standing under a banana tree. Without wasting a minute, I went to him and captured him as a slave. Then I pushed him in front of me, telling him to keep going while I followed closely with my gun and hunting bag. As we were going along, he began to cry, saying that it was his father who had sent him to pluck bananas. As he was saying this, he was not walking very fast, so I cut a small whip and started to lash him along the way. He walked faster when he felt the pain of the whip. At seven o'clock in the evening, when we had reached a certain spot, I told him to stop, and I put my gun and bag down. Then I made a fire under a nearby tree and roasted some yams, which both of us ate. Afterwards I swept that spot and told this young ghost to sleep in a certain place in the clearing. I took my gun and hunting bag, carried them to a secret place and hid them there. When I returned, I laid down behind the young ghost, and within a few minutes I was fast asleep.

I woke suddenly at midnight and discovered that this young ghost had run away. With great fear I ran to the place where I had hidden my gun and bag, but I was relieved to find that the young ghost had not escaped with them. At dawn I chewed my chewing stick, ate some bananas and a small kolanut, and drank some water. At eight o'clock I continued my journey.

At 2:30 in the afternoon I heard people playing something like football and blowing something like a whistle somewhere nearby. I hesitated, listening to these strange noises and then thought I heard the shouts of school boys. I started to travel to the part of the bush from which these strange noises were coming. After a while I arrived at a big town.

On entering this town, I felt very ashamed of my dirty body and dirty clothes because ever since I had entered this bush against my will six years earlier, I had not bathed or washed my clothes once. To my great surprise, I saw that all the ghosts of this town were in white clothes. Their town was also very clean. They were very surprised to see me too.

I saw many children playing something like football. Since they were far away from me, I went to them. I met a lady with them whom I took to be their school mistress, and after we had greeted one another, she took me to her house. On seeing my dirty body, she told her servant to prepare a bath for me, and I washed my body thoroughly. Meanwhile this kind lady took my dirty clothes, gun and hunting bag and locked them in one of her rooms. Then she gave me another set of clothes to wear and told her servant to set food on the table for me. I ate to my entire satisfaction for I had never tasted such nice food since entering this

Bush of the Ghosts. Afterwards she invited me to enter her bedroom and sleep there, and I enjoyed the sleep as well because I had never slept in such a comfortable place since I had started wandering about in this Bush of the Ghosts. When she later noticed that I had woken up, she told her servant to prepare another kind of food for me and I enjoyed that thoroughly as well.

At seven o'clock in the evening I heard the loud sound of a church bell, and this lady suggested that we go to church for the evening prayer. When we returned to the house, we ate dinner together and began a conversation. She asked my name and I told her that I was called "Joseph Adday." She was very glad when she heard my first name was Joseph because she loved all names that were related to religion. She asked which church I was attending in my town before I entered the Bush of the Ghosts, and I told her that it was called "The African Church." She also asked me how I managed to enter the Bush of the Ghosts, and I explained briefly that I was a hunter and that while hunting in a bush I had climbed a tree to keep myself away from scorpions and other creatures. I had fallen asleep heedlessly on top of that tree, and the ghost who was living inside it had carried both the tree and me into this Bush of the Ghosts. Since then I had been searching for the road back to my town, but I hadn't been able to find it. She asked me whether I had died in my town before I entered the Bush of the Ghosts and I replied that I had not.

After asking all these questions, she started to tell me her story thus: "I was born in South Africa long ago. My father and mother came from an unknown land and settled in South Africa in the year 1800. I was born three years later. My parents brought "The Salvation Army Church" here, and I was baptized in this church seven days after I was born. The names given to me on that day were 'Victoria Juliana.'

"When I was eight years old, I started to go to church with my parents and started to learn how to do the work of God. One day, when I was just twelve years old, I fell downstairs, and though I was taken to the hospital immediately, I died three days later as a result of the injuries I received. It made me sad, for my mother had bought many beautiful dresses for me for the Easter festival that year. My parents buried me with those dresses.

"Of course, the third day after my burial I was resurrected, and I went to the entrance of the heaven in order to pass through the gates. The officers in charge of the entrance stopped me, asking me to produce my certificate of baptism. When they took it from me, they went with it to their records office, examined all the records, and saw that I had died too early. They told me that I should go back to my town or anywhere I liked. I waited and begged them for three weeks to allow me to pass into heaven, but they refused. Then I left them and came to settle in this fourth town of the ghosts.

"Of course, this fourth town was very small at that time. At first I started to preach the sermons of God to the ghosts who were in front of my house. Other ghosts heard that the sermons were good and they too began to come to my house to hear them. Even ghosts from neighboring bushes settled here in order to listen to my everyday sermons. Finally, when I saw that the ghosts were quite numerous, I built "The Salvation-Army Church." It contained about nine hundred ghosts.

"As time went on, I started to teach the children of these ghosts how to read and write their language.

By then the number of ghosts in this town had increased to 896,000, and the town had extended to about seven miles square. I was exceedingly glad when you told me that your name is Joseph Adday, and I shall be happy to start to teach you the work of God and to teach you how to read and write the language of ghosts." It was thus that this Juliana related her story to me.

Now my mind was at rest as soon as I began to live with Juliana, and I did not think of going back to my town any more. I had never had an opportunity to learn to read or write before I came to her, so I continued to attend her school, even though the rest of the scholars there were ghosts. To my surprise, sometimes during school hours these ghost scholars would disappear suddenly to an unknown place. Then Juliana and I would remain alone in the school. I never saw the ghost scholars return but I heard their noises and then I would see them again in the classrooms. One day when I noticed that they had disappeared again, I asked Juliana why the ghost scholars were disappearing like that. She told me that since they were ghosts, they could not stay long in one place like human beings.

When Juliana noticed that I was bright in all

subjects, she appointed me as headmaster of the school. Then I began to teach these ghosts how to read and write, and I preached sermons about God. In this school we had sports such as football, cricket, jumping, running, etc. I was very surprised that Juliana knew when Empire Day occurred. We celebrated it every year. Our final examinations used to take place every December 5th, but before the ghost scholars finished their examinations, the Devil used to ask us to send him the names of the scholars who passed so he could employ them.

One day Juliana took me around the town and we paid visits to the school children's parents. I was frightened when I saw one man who had died in my town long ago. In fact, I had been one of the persons who had buried his body. When we saw one another, he wanted to shake hands with me, but I fearfully held my hand back from him. When Juliana saw me do this, she asked me why I did so. I explained to her that the man had died in my town, but she replied that I should not refuse to shake his hand again, for he had the power to change me to one of the deads there. I was greatly shocked.

When we returned to the house, she gave me a map of this fourth town of the ghosts. She told me to take care of it, and I kept it in a safe place. A few days later she invited me to the parlor and told me more about this fourth town. She also gave me a map of the fifth town of the ghosts, explaining that this fifth town was about six hundred miles inside the bush and belonged to Devil, Satan, Traitor, etc. I was unable to sleep well that night because she suddenly started to behave like a dead person.

When I completed eighteen years with her, she invited me to her parlor on a Friday night. She told me to take great care of the house and the school and to continue to preach to the ghosts. Then she took her bed outside the house and bade me goodbye with sorrow. I called to her, asking why she said goodbye, but she did not say anything. I went to bed in fear while she continued lying down on her bed outside of the house. At midnight I heard lovely music coming down from heaven. Different colors of blue, yellow, green and red light were reflected on every part of the house. The music was so melodious that I began to dance on the bed. Everybody else in this town also began to dance, and so did the trees and bushes which surrounded the town. After I had enjoyed the music for fifteen minutes, I heard nothing further, and there were no more lights. Everything became calm suddenly. With fear I stood up and went to the place where Juliana slept outside. She was not there, but I saw a telegram on her bed. When I opened it, I learned that she had left for heaven.

Although she had finally departed, I continued to do all that she had trained me to do. However, these ghosts were not satisfied with what I was doing for them. Their behavior towards me was not encouraging. One day I realized that I was the only human being in the town and that I was living alone in the house which Juliana had left for me. Moreover, I was unable to sleep at night because of the terrible noise of footsteps which I was hearing. It was as if one hundred people were entering and leaving the house. Sometimes these invisible people were walking to and fro, and sometimes the whole house was turning upside down. I became so dejected that on the sixtieth day after Juliana had disappeared to heaven, I opened the room in which she kept my dirty clothes, gun and hunting bag, took everything and wrote this letter to her in heaven:

>
> From: Joseph Adday (Wild Hunter)
>   Headmaster
>   4th Town of the Ghosts
>   Bush of the Ghosts
>   In the year 1838
>
> Dear Miss Victoria Juliana,
>
> I am very sorry to tell you that I am leaving this fourth town of the Ghosts today. My reason for leaving is that the ghosts of this town are not attending church services and the scholars are not attending school. Since they ill-treat me and do not cooperate with me, I am leaving the town peacefully today.
>
> I am yours faithfully,
>
> Joseph Adday
> The Wild Hunter

Then I hung my gun and hunting bag on my left shoulder, and I left this fourth town.

On the Way to the Fifth Town of the Ghosts

It was on the 4th day of May, 1838, that I left the fourth town with tears, and began my journey again, seeking the way to my town. After three months of wandering about in the bush, I met a ghost who was creeping about like a baby. He was a half-bodied ghost, and when I met him, I asked him to show me the road to my town. He said he would show me the road if I would carry him to his mother's house, which was no more than one-quarter of a mile from the spot where I met him. I was so glad that I knelt down immediately, he jumped on my head without hesitation, and I started to carry this half-bodied ghost to his mother's house. This was how I started another journey in this bush.

We did not reach his mother's house immediately. Whenever I missed the way, he showed me the right road, but I became very tired and very hungry for food because I had not eaten anything since morning. I said that I wanted to put him down so that I could find something to eat and also rest for a few minutes, but this ghost shouted terribly, saying that unless I carried him to his mother's house, I would die of hunger. He also refused to come down from my head. I made a greater effort and continued to carry him along, thinking that perhaps his mother's house was not so far from that place. It was later that I knew I had not even carried him halfway to his mother's house.

As we went on our way, he told me very earnestly that he would not allow me to eat or rest until I carried him to his mother's house. "But where is your mother's house?" I shouted with annoyance. "Don't ask that! Just keep going along!" he replied without mercy. However, I became so hungry that with one hand I searched my hunting bag, hoping to find something to eat there. Fortunately I found a dried coco-yam and brought it out, but just when I was trying to throw it into my mouth, this ghost snatched it from my hand unexpectedly, threw it into his own mouth and swallowed it immediately.

Having seen him do so, I became so angry that I started to punish him, even though he was immortal. Carrying him further, I came to a stream that I had to cross, and when I had forded half of it so that the water covered much of my body, suddenly I dived into it with the hope that this ghost would come off from my head. However, to my surprise he began to enjoy the water and even wanted me to stay in the water as long as I could. Since the water had no effect on him, I continued to carry him along.

A few minutes later it came to my mind to run away when he fell asleep at night, but this ghost did not fall asleep. Instead, he started to sing loudly and happily, and as he was singing, he was spitting and discharging urine and excrement onto every part of my body. After a while, when I was fed up with carrying him along, I stopped and jerked myself suddenly, thinking perhaps he would fall off my head. But he held onto my head with his fingernails which were about six inches long. They were as sharp as a knife, and his palms were full of short thorns that were as sharp as sand. He was making several kinds of noise so he sounded like a crowded marketplace. Sometimes he would burst into such loud laughter that a person two miles away would not be able to avoid hearing him. Whenever he met another ghost, he would force me to stop and then he and that ghost would converse for more than two hours. Ah, that was how it was when I was carrying this ghost about in the bush for a good three days without eating or resting once.

However, on the third day that he was on my head, we finally reached his mother's house. As soon as he got off me, he entered the house. I was afraid to leave that place that night for fear that I might fall into the hands of another ghost, so I waited in front of the house.

After a while he told his mother to come out and see me. She looked at me with wonder and went back. When I took a look at her, I saw that she had two heads, one facing backward and the other facing forward. Each head had one large eye and one broad ear.

After ten minutes she brought two uncooked yams to me to eat. Since I could not eat uncooked yams, I gathered dried sticks together, lit them and then roasted the yams in that fire. As soon as I began to eat the yams, all the ghosts living in that house came out to see me. They surrounded me and watched me eating the yams. As soon as I had finished, they returned to the house. I swept that spot, lay down, and as soon as the mother of the half-bodied ghost saw that I slept, she woke me and told me to come inside and sleep. I refused to enter the house because I was sure that if I did, they would never allow me to go out again.

At dawn I called the half-bodied ghost and asked him to show me the road to my town as he had promised to do before I started to carry him about. He refused to do so, saying that he wanted me to live there with him so that I might carry him wherever he wished to go. When he refused to fulfill his promise and when I thought over how I had carried him for three days, I fastened my eyes on him with great annoyance for a few minutes. Then I began to curse him in the name of the god of iron. When his mother heard my curse, she came out and asked me why I was doing that. After I told her the reason, she returned to the house without blaming her son because she was pleased with what her son had told me.

I started to pack my gun, bag and cutlass in order to leave there at once, but the mother came up to me with two wooden ladles which she gave to me, asking me to go and wash them for her in a stream fifty feet from their house. She promised that if I washed them for her, she would tell me the right road to my town. At first I refused to wash the ladles for I thought that she, like her son, might not fulfill her promise. But when I saw that she was an old woman who would not tell a lie, I took the wooden ladles from her. She then warned me that I must not let the water carry the ladles away from me.

When I got to the stream I noticed that it was about seventeen feet wide and that the currents of the flowing water were very strong. However, I entered this stream stopping at its edge. I put one of the two wooden ladles under my foot and pressed it on the ground so that the tide would not carry it away. Then I started to wash the other one. However, when I raised my head up, I saw that the ladle which I had pressed down with my foot had been carried away by the tide. I remembered that the old woman had warned me not to allow this to happen, so I started to follow it, hoping I might catch it. After going about eighty feet, the ladle disappeared entirely.

As I kept moving along on the stream looking for

the ladle, I saw a strange old woman sitting on a block of ice upon the bank of the stream. I asked her if she had seen a wooden ladle carried by the tide, but instead of replying she asked me who gave me the two ladles for washing. When I told her, she simply showed me a garden that was full of fruit trees. The garden was about twenty-five yards away from the block of ice on which she sat. Having pointed out the garden to me, she told me to go there and look for two different kinds of fruit on top of one of the trees. She said that one kind of fruit would be saying "Pluck me! Pluck me! Pluck me!" while the other kind would keep quiet. She cautioned me to pluck only the one that was talking and not the quiet one. To my astonishment, as soon as I entered the garden, I saw one fruit talking while the other one kept quiet. I plucked the one that was saying "Pluck me! Pluck me! Pluck me!" but it stopped talking immediately. When I returned to the old woman and showed her this fruit, she told me to go and throw it on the ground in front of the house in which the mother of the half-bodied ghost lived with her son, the half-bodied ghost, and others. Without hesitation, I left her.

As soon as the mother of the half-bodied ghost saw me approaching, she ran outside asking me for her wooden ladles. I threw the talking fruit on the ground in front of her house, but hardly had it broken into pieces when uncountable small snakes, bees and wasps came out of it. They covered her and everyone who was in the house. The small snakes were biting them and the bees and wasps were stinging them until they disappeared. Seeing all of them go, I thanked God for punishing them in my presence.

Then I took my gun and hunting bag, left the house immediately, and continued to wander about in the bush, looking for the road to my town. Ever since Miss Victoria Juliana had left me for heaven, I had been eager to return to my town. The town plan of the fifth town of ghosts which she gave me before she went to heaven was still with me, but I was not anxious to go to that town. I continued to roam about in this bush for about six months, meeting several ghosts who were quite different from those I had met earlier. These ghosts were even more terrible than the others, but I don't have enough time to describe them fully and tell their stories here.

In February, 1835, I met seven hunters who had been lost for many years in this Bush of the Ghosts. They were my townsfolk. Before they got lost, we had hunted for animals together in the same bush. We were always playing, eating and drinking together. When they had disappeared, their parents had thought that wild beasts had killed them. When I met these lost hunters in the bush, I was exceedingly surprised. I was so glad that I started to jump up and down, for I knew that the ghosts would not be able to harm me any more. Only two months remained before these hunters would turn into real ghosts. In fact, I noticed that they had already turned into half-ghosts. Having greeted one another, we shook hands and laughed together for several minutes. Then I started to ask each of them to tell me how he got to the Bush of the Ghosts.

The first hunter said, "When I was hunting in a certain bush, I got tired, so I climbed an elephant which I took to be a log of wood. As I sat on its back resting, I fell asleep, and before I woke, the elephant had carried me to this Bush of the Ghosts. Since then I have been trying to find my way back to my town, and one day I met the second hunter in this same bush." It was thus the first hunter explained to me how he got lost in this bush. This hunter had mastered the art of killing any kind of animal when he was six years of age.

Then I turned to the second hunter and asked him how he came to this place. He said, "The same dog that found me when the woman who bore me threw me on the roadside when I was one day old, came to me in the bush when I was hunting. The dog turned into a giant in my presence and then brought me to this Bush of the Ghosts. It has been more than forty years now that I have been in this bush. I could not find the way back to town." This second hunter who sadly told me his story had been my close friend before he disappeared. His adopted father's house was near my father's house. He had no mother because he had been brought to this old man's house by the old man's dog when he was just one day old. The old man, having cared for him till he grew up, had adopted him as his son, so the hunter regarded the old man as his father. When he was ten years old, the hunter had more than four hundred dogs which he was using to kill animals. There was no one else who ever lived in this world who had as many charms or spells as he had. He was knowledgeable in every kind of supernatural power.

When the second hunter finished, I turned to the third hunter who had almost wasted away to skin and bones as a result of longing to go home. I asked him how he had entered that Bush of the Ghosts, and he explained to me tearfully that, "I am the only son among my father's children; the rest are daughters. Because I was his only son, my father loved me much more than his daughters, and for this reason those daughters hated me very much. One day when my father was out of town and I was sleeping, those daughters joined hands together and brought me to this bush. They then left me here and went away. When I woke from sleep, I discovered myself here and I could not find my way to the town. That was when I became a hunter." This third hunter had hardly finished his story when he asked me anxiously whether his father and mother were still alive. I told him that they were alive when I left our town but I could not say whether they were alive or dead now because it had been twenty-nine years since I had become lost in this Bush of the Ghosts.

Then I turned to the fourth hunter and asked him how he had entered this bush. He said with a sorrowful voice that, "One day, when I went to a certain bush which was near our town, I saw a strange bird on the top of a tree. When I shot at it, it pounced on me and carried me to this Bush of the Ghosts. While it was carrying me along, I begged it to release me, but it did not listen to me at all. When it put me on the ground, it told me that it would kill me immediately to avenge its own young ones whom I had killed. After I had begged for mercy in the name of God and in the name of the king of birds for many minutes, it told me that it would leave me in this Bush of the Ghosts so the ghosts could put me to death. Then it left me here and flew away at once. Since that day, I have been trying to get out of this Bush of the Ghosts but I have not been able to." I asked him how long he had been there. When he told me it had been fifteen years, I told him that I had been there before him. This fourth hunter was an expert bird killer. He killed only birds and he had killed almost every kind of bird on earth. He had started killing birds as he was growing up. For this he was well-known to both adults and children of our town. Whenever someone was troubled by a witch, this hunter was invited to help kill it, and indeed he used to kill it.

I then turned to the fifth hunter who had already opened his mouth wide to tell me his grief. When I asked him to tell me how he came to the Bush of the Ghosts, he said, "One day, when I went to a bush which was not so far from our town, a strong breeze blowing there blew me into this Bush of the Ghosts. Since that day I have not been able to leave it." The fifth hunter told me this with great sorrow. In fact, there was a strange forest about seventy miles from our town where at a certain time of year a strong breeze used to blow to every part of town. It was so strong that if someone was careless enough to stay outside or in the bush at that time, it would blow him or her far away. This fifth hunter had not done any kind of work except hunting since he was a boy. He was fond of killing such beasts as elephants, tigers, lions, buffaloes, apes and deers.

I turned to the sixth hunter and asked him how he came to this bush. He replied that, "I was a close friend of a spirit who later stole my ammunition and my meat. When I asked him about these things, he gave me two slaps on my ears. Then many other spirits of that bush came out and joined that spirit who stole my ammunition and meat. They all carried me to this Bush of the Ghosts. Since then I have not been able to leave it." In fact, he had been only a small boy when he had started to live in the bush with animals and spirits. He used to hunt such creatures too. The only time that he used to come to town was when his clothes were torn to rags or when his gunpowder was finished.

Then I turned to the seventh hunter and asked him how he had come to the Bush of the Ghosts. He said, "One day when I slept in my room, I started dreaming, and in my dream I saw many wild animals chasing me about and trying to kill me. After a while I became so tired that I fell on the ground. Then the animals in my dream carried me to this Bush of the Ghosts, and indeed, when I woke up, I found myself with my bag of spells and cutlass in this Bush of the Ghosts." This seventh hunter was one of the strongest men in our town. He was much more skilled in the use of charms than anyone else in the town. Both witches and wizards feared his powerful charms. None of the townspeople had ever entered his house since he built it. He did not use a bow, spear, cutlass or any other kind of weapon to kill animals, but he was so versed in charms that he caught such animals as tigers, lions, elephants, jackdaws, etc., alive, and he used to bring them to town alive.

When each of these seven hunters had told me how he had come there, then I, as the Wild Hunter and the eighth hunter, told them as well how I had entered the Bush of the Ghosts. I described the first, second, third and fourth towns of the Ghosts and told them how all the ghosts I had met in those towns had treated me badly. Having informed them of my previous hardships, I showed them the plans of the fourth and fifth towns which Juliana had given to me when her time of going to heaven was imminent. I also told them how I had been educated and had served as the school headmaster. After that, I advised them that it would be better for us to unite and continue to seek a way back to our town, because it was not wise for us to stay in the Bush of the Ghosts and die there. When I suggested this, all of them were pleased except the seventh hunter, who objected to my proposal. He stood up and said that my suggestion was good, but it would be better for us to go to our dead parents in heaven and tell them how we had become lost in the Bush of the Ghosts long ago and could not find our way back to our town. Perhaps our dead parents would allow us to live with them there, whereas if we pinned our hopes on getting back to our town, we might simply perish in the Bush of the Ghosts.

When the seventh hunter told us his opinion, the rest of us agreed. At this stage I brought out the map of the fifth town of the Ghosts again and spread it on the ground. All of us squatted, fastening our eyes on it. We saw that there was no road to heaven except through this fifth town, so in August, 1838, we started our journey toward the fifth town. After having travelled for two months, we stopped and built a small temporary house on the roadway leading to the fifth town. During the nine months we lived in this house, we planted corn so we would have a good supply of food during the rest of our journey. As soon as the corn was ripe we harvested it, and put it all in our hunting bags. The first, second and sixth hunters then put these loads on their heads and we continued on our way. As we were travelling along, many ghosts saw us and followed us, begging us to give them our corn to eat. They were nearly dying of hunger because food was rare in that area and all the ghosts there were lazy. But we did not give them any of our corn.

The Fifth Town of the Ghosts

Ten months after we had started our journey, we arrived at the gate of the fifth town. It was two o'clock p.m. The gate-keeper stopped us and asked us where we were going. When we told him that we were going to see the king of the fifth town who was called Devil, he told us to surrender our guns to him. As soon as we did so, he opened the gate for us, and we passed through to this town. As we continued to travel along in that town, we saw two soldiers standing side by side on a pillar that was about ten feet high. Both of them resembled human beings but they were not. The pillar on which they stood was in the center of the main road which went directly to heaven. This road was at the south end of the town, and crowds of people were travelling on it. We branched off when we saw "Devil Street" written on a broad board that was hung on a big pillar standing by the roadside. As we travelled down Devil Street, we noticed that every house was numbered. We went past sixteen houses before we came to Devil's palace, the number of which was 986666656 D. We entered the palace and asked for "His Majesty the King of Hell."

When we were told that he was in his office, we asked that someone take us there, and one of his ambassadors led us to the office immediately. There I met many of my old pupils who were educated in the school in the fourth town where I was headmaster. All of them were employed in the office of the Devil. Without hesitation and with great happiness one of those boys took us to the Devil in his private office. After we had greeted one another, the Devil asked us to sit in front of him. The Devil then greeted us once more, but this time hot flames came out of his mouth, and we were unable to answer. Instead we were startled and stood up suddenly in great confusion. When we sat down again, we did so fearfully, ready to run away should hot flames come out of his mouth again.

Our First Day in the Fifth Town

On our first day in the fifth town the Devil asked us where we came from. We replied with fear that we came from earth. Then he asked us what we came to him for. We replied that we came for the purpose of seeing the kind of work that he was doing there. When he asked us to tell him our names, we said that each of us was called "Devil's-helper." We feared to tell him our real names or to tell him that we were hunters because we thought he might put us into his hellfires. Promising that he would show us every part of his town later, he commanded one of his servants to take us to the rest house where we were given one large room and servants. This mighty room was more than twenty feet by twenty feet. The two servants soon brought us fine food, drinks and raw tobacco, and we ate to our satisfaction. We could not drink the drinks at all because they were too strong for us. When the third hunter dipped his finger into this type of drink just to taste a bit of it, his finger was simply burnt off as if it was a piece of paper. We were unable to smoke the raw tobacco as well. The first hunter who lit some tobacco fainted immediately, as did some of the rest of us who smelt even a small bit of the smoke from this raw tobacco. At eight o'clock at night the Devil visited us in our room and talked to us for some minutes. When he returned to his palace, we slept.

Our Second Day in the Fifth Town

At eight o'clock in the morning, we went to the Devil's office. When we got there, he told one of his clerks to take us round the town and show us all the important things that were there. He was so busy that morning that he was unable to take us round the town by himself as he had promised to do. As we went round the town, we saw that it was beautiful, but the people there were as bad as their king the Devil. All held knives, spears, bows and arrows, and many other dangerous weapons, and were going about in the streets restless in mind. Sometimes they stopped and started to fight one another. Both children and grown-ups there had long fingernails and were as dirty as their king the Devil. Their heads were entirely covered with dirty hair so it was very hard to see their eyes and faces. To our surprise, we did not see any of these people laugh; they were just walking and fighting one another sadly as if they were in deep mourning. These people liked to be in fire more than in water. We even saw several of them living inside the fire. We noticed as well that rain never fell there all the year round. Then we returned to our large room and ate our food.

Our Third Day in the Fifth Town

The following morning we visited the Devil's soldiers in their barracks one and a half miles from the town. Afterwards the commander of the Devil's army took us into his office and showed us the list of serving soldiers who numbered 188 million; the recruits numbered over 1,000 million. The commander told us that they were preparing to engage still more recruits until there were as many as 986,800 million. Having seen all those things, we returned to our room.

Fourth Day in the Fifth Town

The following morning we visited the Devil's engineering department where the hellfires were. There we saw the kind of firemen we had never seen anywhere in the world. There was not a human being who could stand half a mile away and look at them. No one could approach them either. They were turned to the fire, and wherever they stood, that place would start to burn immediately. The Devil had built their living quarters near the hellfires. These firemen used to stop work at 4:30 in the evening. Then they would go and bathe in a large deep river not too far from the engineering department. The fire on their bodies used to boil the water of the deep river as soon as they started to bathe in it. The work of these firemen was to put coals inside the bottomless hearths of the hellfires and then to carry ashes away.

Later, when we were taken to the other side of this hellfire, we noticed that there were three more hellfires there. Coals and a kind of thick oil were used in the first of the three. Those who were working there were living in the oil. The second of the three was reserved for all the ghosts of the Bush of the Ghosts, and it was 1986 miles deep. The third was for the Devil and had no bottom at all. In this way we learned that there were four hellfires in this engineering department.

The burning materials used in the Devil's own hellfire were flinty stones instead of coals because the fire had to burn continuously. We saw as well that many houses were built with stones inside this fourth hell. When we asked the man showing us the hellfires about the Devil's palace, he told us that those living inside it at that time were the Devil's father, mother and aunts. Then we asked how many firemen were working there. He said that there were more than forty-eight thousand. When we asked when the Devil was going to live in the fourth hellfire, he told us that it would become the Devil's permanent home on "judgement-day" which was coming soon.

Our Fifth Day in the Fifth Town

We visited all the Devil's offices the following day. The first was the correspondence section and we saw uncountable clerks working there. Then we visited the Labor Headquarters and met the Commissioner of Labor in his office. His name was called Death and he was the Devil's cousin. Next we went to the Office of the Exchange Manager whose name was Blasphemer. This Exchange Manager was happy to take us to the Exchange Office where we saw all the records of sinners, both those who were ghosts and those who were people on earth. He showed us as well the names and numbers of sinners who had been in the fire for the past six hundred years. Everyone's behavior was recorded in red ink. The Exchange Manager told us further that if someone's record was not found in their office, it meant that he or she was in heaven.

As we were looking at those records, the Manager asked us to tell him our names. To our surprise, after he had checked the records for a while, he brought out those that belonged to the second hunter, fourth hunter and seventh hunter. When he opened each of these, he told us that those three hunters would go to the fires of hell in the future. Then he looked for the records of the first hunter, the third hunter, the fifth hunter, and me, the eighth hunter, but he did not find them there, so he told us that we had no sin at all. But he hinted at the same time that he was afraid the records of the sixth hunter would be sent to their office soon from earth.

I was exceedingly glad when he did not find my records in their office there, but I was sorry for those three hunters whose records were found. They began to weep as soon as they heard that they definitely would be coming to the fires of hell. We also saw there the records of many people of our town who were bad before they died. The Exchange Manager explained to us that if someone was going to die in ten years' time, they would receive his record before that time. Only a few people would join God in heaven. All the rest would go to hell.

After he had shown us the records, we went to the Office of the Chief Secretary of hell. After chatting with us for a few minutes, he stood up and led us to his staff offices where we saw thousands of clerks. They were very busy working out schemes to trick more people into coming to hell. They gave us a warm welcome. After he had shown us several interesting and fearful things, the Chief Secretary returned to his office, and we returned to our room as well.

Our Sixth Day in the Fifth Town

On our sixth day we called upon the Devil in his office again. We told him happily that we had visited all his departments and had seen his works. Then I started to ask him questions: "Your Majesty, who will live in the fourth hell?" "Ah, the fourth hell is for me and my followers," the Devil replied fearlessly. "Your Majesty, the king of hells, what are you going to do with your soldiers?" I asked him. "I want all the people of the world to be my followers and to follow me to hell. That is why I have got my soldiers ready to fight all the people who refuse to follow me to number four hell, but the soldiers are not to kill them. I am not going to live in that fire alone." The Devil explained this to us laughing, as if hellfire was cold water to him. Then I asked, "But what are you doing with the two fearful images of soldiers which stand in the middle of the main road to your town?" "Those two images of soldiers are to commemorate the fierce fight which I had with God when I was in heaven. God later defeated me, and then He drove me from His heaven to this fifth town of the ghosts to be the controller of all the hells here. Those two images honor soldiers who, when they were alive, helped me greatly to fight God," the Devil told us with great confidence. "But in what year were you born?" I asked the Devil. "I was born at a time when the year was yet at zero. Since I was born inside fire, fire is just as cold as ice to my body," the Devil replied cheerfully. "In what year do you expect to die?" I asked fearlessly. "Ah, only the Day of Judgement will determine the day of my death. At present my record shows that I will be in the everlasting fire of the fourth hell," he said simply.

Then, in return, the Devil asked us the kind of work we were doing on earth before coming to him. We all replied in unison that we were his followers while we were on earth. We also lied further by saying that we were hearing his name everywhere in the world. His name was so well-known to everyone that we started our journey to come and see him with our own eyes as if he were our father. When the Devil heard so from us, he jumped up high suddenly with a happiness that cannot be described. He shouted so loud that every part of the fifth town and the four hells shook, and several houses in the town collapsed. All the people on the streets were afraid and hid themselves in any place they could find. The birds in the sky fell on the ground, and all the fish in the ocean came out to see who shouted. Many mighty trees fell down, and the mountains which surrounded the fifth town sunk into the ground unexpectedly. And we, the eight hunters who stood before him, fainted for many minutes before we regained consciousness.

Ah! reader of this story, the Devil is the most powerful being in this world, and he greatly loves any person who claims to be one of his followers. We had hardly become conscious when His Majesty, the Devil and king of hell, happily went on to tell us the rest of his story. He told us earnestly, "You see, sons of man, that I am the king and father of hell, so you, my followers, will be my sons in hell. Ah, I am very happy to hear from you today that all the people of the world are hearing much about me and that you eight men came to visit me, your father, in this fifth town of the ghosts. I am sure now that I shall get nearly all the people of the world to be with me in hell. I am the Devil, the mighty, who fought with the God who created me and everything else. But Almighty God defeated me and drove me from His heaven to this fifth town. He defeated me simply because I had only a few soldiers or followers at that time. But now I am sure the number of my followers is increasing rapidly, and by your power the number will continue to increase more and more. Anyone who follows God is my enemy, but anyone who follows me will be my son, and I shall be his father. I shall love him as I love myself. I am the king of hell but I will be the last one to go there. My father, mother and aunts are living there at present. On the Judgement Day I am very sure that fire will be my food and drink, and I shall be bathing in fire as a man bathes in a big river. I am certain that I shall never come out of the fire. Though I shall not die, I shall not burn into ashes! Ah, my followers, that is the day that you and I shall wear fire like clothes, but I alone shall wear the crown of fire that big day because I am your father and king! Everything I am telling you now is true and nothing can change it!" That was how the Devil told us the story of everything that would happen to him and his followers in the future.

Although we were not his true followers, we were so depressed that we thanked him sadly. That morning we noticed that the Devil decorated his office with guns, spears, bows and arrows, matchets, axes, and many other dangerous weapons. We noticed as well that his smoking pipe was about four feet long, and its bowl contained more than a ton of tobacco at a time. There were about fifty men who had no other work than to load tobacco into the bowl of that pipe and to clear away the ashes of the burnt tobacco. That was their job every day. There was a big chimney in his office through which the smoke of his pipe was passing outside.

In order to see these wonderful and fearful things, we went round the fifth town once more. We came to one street named "Devil Street," the longest and widest of all the streets there. "Hell Street" started from the center of the town and ended in the front of the Hell Engineering Department. "Woe Street" was also long, but shorter than "Devil Street"; of course, it went along the commercial area. "Judas Street" and "Traitor Street" were the shortest.

Once Devil had heard that we were his followers,

he told us that he would send us for six months of training in his school, which was called "Devil's Training Center for Punishments." When we told him that we agreed to go for training, he sent us to the principal of the school. There we were taught how to persuade those who obeyed God to disobey Him and to follow the Devil instead. After six months of training, the principal of the school tested us. Many of us passed, but I, the Wild Hunter or the 8th hunter, failed because I so hated to be a follower of the Devil that I did not pay heed to the training. After we completed our training, the principal sent us back to the Devil.

We were deeply shocked when we saw that the records of the first and fifth hunters had come to the records office from earth. When both hunters learned this, they started to weep bitterly, and within a few hours they had wasted away to bare bones. We other hunters mourned bitterly with them, but this did not help in any way. The following day the Exchange Manager sent for these hunters and showed their records to them. Again these two hunters jumped up high, fell flat on the floor, and burst into tears. The rest of us joined them in weeping so noisily that the whole building was full of sorrowful sounds. When this was too much for the Exchange Manager, he told us to go back to our big room. We all wept bitterly throughout that day.

The following morning we went to the Devil and told him that we would go to heaven to lure several angels of God to him. When he heard this, he was so glad that he gave us a map of the road which went to heaven. We thanked him and promised that we would not stay too long in heaven before returning to him. This was how we deceived him. However, he detained in the fifth town the first, second, fourth, fifth and seventh hunters because their records had been found in his records office. That meant they were sinners. Of course, he promised that he would send them to his Engineering Department for employment and that he would offer them high posts. Before we started our journey, and while the Devil was not looking for a few minutes, we advised the five hunters to follow us to heaven, but they refused, saying sorrowfully that once their records were found in the Devil's office, God would turn them back from heaven because sinners could not be with Him.

    Before we left the Devil and his fifth town of the Ghosts that morning, the Devil assured us that anyone who was anxious to know whether his or her record was in his office could write to him and ask. He said that if the records of such a person were in his office, he would reply immediately, but if the record was not available in his office, then he would forward the letter to the record office in heaven without delay. The Devil told us further that as soon as he received a reply from heaven, he would forward it to the person immediately. The Devil suggested that the person should use two envelopes. He or she should write his or her name and address on the back of one of the two envelopes, and the correct postage stamp should be affixed to it. After that, the second envelope should be addressed as follows:

        To His Majesty the King of Hell
        17896 Woe Lane
        5th Town of the Ghosts
        Bush of the Ghosts
        HELL

After addressing the second envelope, the person should put his or her letter inside it, gum it well, and post it to hell. But the person should bear in mind that his or her original record would not be sent but only a copy of it. To make things easy and fast, a postal order or money order for five shillings should be sent with the letter to the "Wild Hunter" who would help the person. As soon as the Devil had told us this, we left his fifth town of the Ghosts. That was in the year 1842.

Our Way to Heaven

As we were travelling along the road, I brought out from my pocket the map that Miss Victoria Juliana gave to me when she was about to leave for heaven. We started to compare it with the one that the Devil gave us. In this way we could be sure that we were on the right road. Though this road was about four feet wide and twenty feet deep, it was as straight as railway lines. This straight road helped us to travel many miles on the day that we started our journey. At about five o'clock that evening we stopped, put our bags down on the roadside, and ate whatever we found near there. Afterwards we slept at that spot. But at midnight we were much troubled by wild animals who, having seen us there, started to prowl up and down, hoping to eat us. Alas! We had no guns with which to shoot these wild animals because the gateman of the fifth town had seized them the day we wanted to enter the town. But we were happy when we learned that these wild animals did not kill people who had no sins or those whose records had not yet been sent to the records office of the Devil. For this reason the animals did not attempt to kill us.

The following morning at about seven o'clock we continued our journey. At twelve o'clock we stopped under the shadow of trees near that road. Having eaten whatever we found around there and rested for two hours, we continued on our way. When it was about six o'clock, we counted the number of miles that we had travelled since leaving the fifth town; it was one hundred and seventeen in all. We saw that our journey was much faster than we expected it to be, but this was because there was no sun shining on this road and it was quite smooth. After estimating the number of miles we had travelled that day, we stopped and rested on the roadside till midnight. Then we continued our journey comfortably throughout the night because there was a clear moon shining on the road.

Since we had covered so many miles by travelling at night, we were tired and decided to stop and rest for eight days inside a valley called "Human Skeletons Valley." We even attended Sunday services with those skeletons in their church. The "Human Skeletons Valley" was a town with a population of about seventeen thousand. Those skeletons, when standing up and walking, were just like living human beings but they had no muscle, only bones. In the daytime these skeletons became entirely lifeless; they would not talk or make any motion whatsoever. All of them would just remain in whatever position suited them. Some would stand, some would lay down, and some would remain motionless on the tops of trees when dawn came. There they would remain until nightfall. Because of this, their town was as calm as a graveyard from morning till night, but they would come alive, talk, shout and move here and there as soon as it was night. They would hold their meetings and visit one another only at night. Their children and domestic animals were skeletons as well. In this town there was no light at all until we left there, but we noticed a large bright light from the sky which used to light up the whole town every night. When we begged these skeletons to give us some food to eat, they were so greedy and stingy that they refused to give us even a drop of water. We left their town in August.

We continued our journey and travelled for five months before we made another rest stop. By then our food was completely exhausted. We came to another valley about 46,000 miles long, twenty feet deep, and six feet wide, and we entered it with fear, looking for something to eat. A messenger from the fifth town came far behind us, shouting and telling us that the Exchange Manager had sent him to get the sixth hunter to return to the fifth town. He told us that the record of the sixth hunter had been received just after we left and it showed that he was a sinner. Therefore he had to return and stay with the Devil. The messenger kept shouting but we did not answer his call nor did the sixth hunter go to him. After waiting at the entrance of the valley for about two hours, the messenger returned to the Exchange Manager. He did not attempt to enter the valley because sinners were forbidden to enter it and he was a sinner.

However, we went on travelling in this valley, and after a while it was revealed to us that this was the "Valley of Sinners," a valley out of bounds to all sinners. This was a very serious obstacle for sinners who were going to heaven. We travelled along in it as fast as we could, but when we were about halfway through it, four long horns sprouted from the sixth hunter's head unexpectedly. Each of the horns was large and up to nine feet long. Two were at the left temple and another two at the right temple. We continued our journey but felt horrified and very depressed. After another mile each of his four horns had grown to eighteen feet, and they soon reached a length of twenty feet. The two at his left temple curved just like a sickle and so did the two at his right temple. Suddenly the four curved horns hooked both walls of this "Valley of Sinners," and the sixth hunter could move neither to his front or back nor to his left or right.

We were not aware of this as we ran forward far away from him, and when we fastened our eyes on him, we shouted with fear, "But who are you?" "I am the same sixth hunter! Please do not leave me here and go away!" the sixth hunter said sorrowfully as he looked at us sternly. But we were so perplexed and worried that we could not pay heed to his sorrowful appeal. We just stood looking at him sluggishly and speechlessly for many minutes. When he saw that we did not respond to his appeal, he shouted again, "Please don't be afraid but come near me and pull me away from the walls of this valley! Please save me!" In fact, we could not leave him hanging up there and go away, so we went to him and began to pull him with all our power. We thought we might be able to set him free from the walls so he could follow us. But after pulling him for many minutes, we saw that his arms and neck were about to tear away from his body, so we left him there for the snakes to kill.

We resumed our journey full of grief. Of course none of the rest of us had known before we entered this "Valley of Sinners" that this sixth hunter was a sinner. When we were in the fifth town, the Exchange Manager had hinted to us about his sin, but we did not believe the Manager at all. That was how we lost one of our group in the "Valley of Sinners." We heard later that he was killed by the snakes, and the wild animals ate his body up.

No sooner had we left the sixth hunter there to his fate but I started to touch my head with fear, wondering if perhaps horns had sprouted there as they had on the sixth hunter. Now only two of us remained, the third hunter and myself. We travelled in this valley for four and a half years before we reached the end of it.

Having left the "Valley of Sinners" behind, we travelled for another eight years before we came to a high and vast mountain. This mountain was so high that if a man looked at its peak with a cap on his head, the cap would fall off. Later we understood that it was from the peak of this mountain that a breeze was blowing to every part of the world. This breeze had to continue non-stop or else all the living creatures of the world would die of suffocation within one second. Without hesitation we started to climb this mountain, but it took us about seven years before we reached its peak.

When we were descending on the other side, we saw creatures whose bodies resembled those of human beings except they had heads just like those of she-goats. Nevertheless, they were very kind to travellers and fed us with rich food throughout the period we spent with them. They spoke fluently like us and their behavior was identical to ours, so it is difficult to describe them. Later we learned that they were among the traitors who betrayed Jesus Christ when He was on earth. We left these half-human, half-she-goat creatures, having spent five comfortable years with them.

Then we descended the mountain and continued our journey. We travelled one hundred miles before we observed that we had missed our way by travelling to the left instead of to the right. The reason for this was that the map of heaven which Juliana gave to me before she left the earth had become so old and torn into so many pieces that we could not see anything on it. Also, the map that the Devil gave us was with the sixth hunter who had already perished in the "Valley of Sinners."

We travelled for one year on this wrong road before we came to a town. When we greeted the people there, they did not reply, but as soon as we started to walk about in the town, we noticed that both the people and their animals were quiet. None of them talked or made any noise whatsoever. Later it was revealed to us that they and their domestic animals such as fowls, goats, sheep, dogs, horses, etc. were talking for only one minute a year. They would become dumb again as soon as the minute expired. It was like that every year. However, since we had missed our road and since we got very good accommodations and food there, we decided to stop our journey and stay there for some time. But to our astonishment the very day that we completed one year there, the time of talking came for these dumb people. It was at this moment that we suddenly heard a lot of noise of people and their domestic animals. We immediately started to go to those who were not far from us, hoping to ask them to show us the right road to heaven. But by the time we came to them, these people and their domestic animals had stopped talking because one minute had already expired. We shouted, asking them to tell us the right road to heaven but they did not reply at all.

We decided that we would continue to stay there for another year until they would talk again. If we ran faster to them at that time to ask them the road to heaven, perhaps they would be able to tell us before one minute had expired. But to our horror, when we had stayed in this town for another three months, the two of us became dumb too. We could not talk to one another at all. Seeing this, we made signs with our hands to each other and agreed to pack our belongings and leave the town at once. That was how we left this town and went back to the same wrong road. Fortunately, after we had continued our journey for two weeks, we were able to talk as usual. The two of us then became very lively. Later we learned that the name of that town was "Dumb Town."

After roaming about for fifteen months, we came to the road that went to heaven and continued our journey on it. We travelled for ten years before we got close to heaven, but we were still sixteen miles away when melodious songs came into our hearing. We had never heard this kind of song in our lives. The songs were so melodious that the third hunter and I unconsciously started to dance along madly. Although we were terribly hungry for food before we heard the songs, we suddenly forgot our hunger. Two hours later we danced madly up to heaven's gate.

We became conscious again when the gate-keepers stopped us, asking, "Where are the two of you going?" "We are going to our dead parents and Miss Victoria Juliana!" I replied with a tired voice. "Had you both died in your town before coming to heaven?" the gate-keepers asked. "No! we had not died before coming," I replied. "Well, if you have not died, you should go back to your town, because those who have not returned their mud-bodies to the earth (mud), are not allowed to pass through this gate to heaven," the gate-keepers explained to us mercilessly. Having heard this, we started to beg them to allow us to pass in. We told them of our past hardships and punishments in the Bush of the Ghosts, in the fifth town, etc., but they refused to allow us to pass into heaven. They simply said, "No person can enter heaven except one who is free from sin." When they said so, I told them that they should go and look at our records. The third hunter and I then started to shout loudly, "Please have mercy on us!" One of them went to the officers who were keeping the records on all the people in the world. He asked for our records and saw that though we were not sinners, we had not yet returned our mud-bodies to the mud, which meant that we were not dead.

Before that gate-keeper returned to us, the third hunter and I had ample time to study the records office. Over eight hundred officers were keeping the records. Many new records were coming in, alerting the officers that many people had just died and would soon be arriving there. When the gate-keeper returned to us, he told his colleagues that our records were good but that we had not died in our town before coming to heaven. Instead of allowing us to go in, they shouted at us to go back to our town and come to them when we were dead. We continued to beg them until Miss Victoria Juliana in heaven heard our voices. She sent a letter to the gate-keepers explaining that both of us were coming to her, so they should allow us to pass into heaven. Then they opened the gate for us and we passed in at once. Thus we reached heaven at last, but it was a great grief to us that of our eight hunters, only two of us reached there.

Our First Day in Heaven

Our first day in heaven we noticed that heaven was the most beautiful of all places. Heavenly orchestras were uncountable, and as a result every part of heaven was always full of melodious music. All the musicians in these orchestras were angels. We saw that there was no darkness at all in heaven; the glory of God was shining on everything continuously. Juliana had sent her heaven address to me when I was in the fourth town, so we were able to go directly to her. When she saw me, she was exceedingly happy, and she immediately welcomed us to her house which was shining in a very lovely way with the glory of God. All the lights in heaven were in glorious technicolor. We ate and then started to enjoy the lovely music being played in every part of heaven by the angels.

Our Second Day in Heaven
Miss Victoria Juliana took us to several parts of heaven, among which were the places from which the sun and moon were rising. We also went to a mighty church ten miles wide and twenty miles long, the walls of which were pure diamond, the roof coral and the pews shining gold.

Our Third Day in Heaven
We visited the angels who in their gorgeous glory were singing songs of praise to God continuously. One of them lifted up the globe of the earth with one hand. Since this was strange to us, we asked Juliana, "Why does this angel hold up the earth?" She explained, "The angel holds up the earth so it will not fall on the ground. In the end the earth is going to fall and break to pieces." "Why?" we asked earnestly, fastening our eyes on her. "People on earth are committing more and more sins. As soon as their sins fill the measure

to its brim, God will tell the angel to drop the globe onto the ground. Then it will break to pieces and so will the sinners. The sinners will go into the everlasting fire while the earth will remain forever," Juliana explained to us in brief.

Our Fourth Day in Heaven

We visited all the prophets who were once on earth. These included Job, Abraham, Noah, Joel, Joseph, etc., whom we met in a glory which cannot be described, and their happiness was without end. Contentment was visible in their eyes. The glory that God gave to each of them was so great that it was overflowing and dropping from his body.

Our Fifth Day in Heaven

We visited a yard in which we saw thousands of angels molding people. The yard was about four thousand miles square. We saw plainly that each person molded from the earth of heaven (dust) was just like a baby one day old. Each was no more than one foot tall. At this early stage they did not talk, but on the morning of their seventh day they would start to talk and walk about in this yard. On the morning of their eighth day they would go to the children's records office, and the angels in charge there would give each of them a name which would be written on the back cover of his record papers.

Our Sixth Day in Heaven

Then Juliana took us to our dead parents who were in heaven with her. They were extremely happy when they saw us, but we had hardly sat down when they asked us for news of our town and of the world. We told them a bit of news, but we had left our town and the world so many years before that we did not know much about it any longer. With great sorrow we told them everything that had happened to us in the Bush of the Ghosts before we reached heaven. When we said we did not want to return to earth but would prefer to live with them there in heaven, they and Juliana shouted at us, "Ah, that is forbidden! You must return to earth, and when you are dead, then you may come back to us!" Having heard this from them, the third hunter and I raised our heads, wondering how we could reach earth and then find our town. Both of us became so dejected that we were unable to stand up. We just burst into tears. As we wept loudly, Juliana shouted horribly at us, "Eh, stop that! There is no weeping or hissing or grief or mourning or suffering in heaven. Let us continue our visit!" Then she suddenly pulled us up and dragged us outside.

As soon as we heard the melodious music the angels were playing, we forgot our sorrow at once and became cheerful -- so cheerful that we forgot all about our parents. Juliana took us to the Reverend D. Williams, Reverend Henry Townsend, Bishop Crowther, etc., who died soon after Jesus left the world. These people gave us presents of Bibles and song books, and we saw the high glory with which God honored them. This glory was so great that when we fastened our eyes on them, we did not know that we had opened our mouths so wide that we were dropping spit. When we were about to leave them, we were lucky enough to be infected by some of their glory. We did not know the reason why this was so. It may have been because we had no sin before we came to heaven. We shouted, "Ah, there is no place like heaven, and when we return to earth, we will advise everyone to keep to his or her religion with untainted faith." We saw plainly that in heaven there were no funerals, deaths, quarrels, hunger, sickness, courts of law or prosecution, prison-yards, etc. The third hunter and I decided we would tell people on earth about all those things that Miss Victoria Juliana showed us when she took us around heaven.

We leave Heaven on the Seventh Day

Miss Victoria Juliana woke us up on the morning of our seventh day in heaven and told us to pack our hunting bags and gifts. After we had done so, she opened the door of a room and told us to enter it with our belongings. To our surprise, we had hardly entered that room when we found ourselves back at the place on earth we had left when we were youths. It was midnight there and not morning as it was in heaven. We thanked God greatly and also thanked Miss Victoria Juliana whom God had sent to help us return to our town safely. Thus I, the Wild Hunter, had gone to hunt animals in the Bush of the Ghosts, which no hunter had ever entered and returned from, but I returned safely after many years of wandering.

Our parents and the other people of our town could not recognize us any more. Many of them had died, and many were so old that they had even forgotten our names. A few of them remembered us faintly when we described ourselves to them. Some said that they thought we were no longer alive. They asked us about the rest of the hunters, and we told them that the first, second, fourth, fifth, sixth and seventh hunters were in the custody of His Majesty the Devil whose palace was in the fifth town of the Ghosts. We explained that the sixth hunter followed us on our journey to heaven but his head sprouted four horns in the "Valley of Sinners." These horns got hooked in the walls of the Valley, and he perished there because he was a sinner.

Alas, our people did not understand what was meant by the fifth town of the Ghosts. We explained that the Bush of the Ghosts was the reserved bush in which both ghosts and spirits of the dead were living as if in their own town. We explained further that though this bush seemed just like an ordinary bush, indeed it was not. Once one entered it, it was not easy to find a way out. One could not travel to the end of it; that was as impossible as it would be for a mosquito to travel around the whole world without perishing. This was how we explained the Bush of the Ghosts to our people.

When the dawn broke, we saw the people of our town with our own eyes, and they too saw us. The bit of glory that had infected us from our contact with the Reverend D. Williams, the Reverend Henry Townsend, Bishop Crowther, etc., faded away from us suddenly. We were told later that the glory of heaven could not remain in us once we were back in this earth of sins. "Ah, it is a pity that this glory has left us!" the third hunter and I exclaimed with great sorrow that morning.